P9-DIB-634

RANDOM
HOUSE
LARGE
PRINT

CLASS ACT

Also by Stuart Woods
Available from Random House Large Print

Jackpot (A Teddy Fay Novel)
Double Jeopardy (A Stone Barrington Novel)
Hush-Hush (A Stone Barrington Novel)
Shakeup (A Stone Barrington Novel)
Choppy Water (A Stone Barrington Novel)
Bombshell (A Teddy Fay Novel)
Hit List (A Stone Barrington Novel)

CLASS ACT

STUART WOODS

RANDOM HOUSE
LARGE PRINT

This is a work of fiction. Names, characters, places, and incidents either are the product of the author's imagination or are used fictitiously, and any resemblance to actual persons, living or dead, businesses, companies, events, or locales is entirely coincidental.

 Published in the United States of America by Random House Large Print in association with G. P. Putnam's Sons, an imprint of Penguin Random House LLC.

The Library of Congress has established a Cataloging-in-Publication record for this title.

ISBN: 978-0-593-41787-4

www.penguinrandomhouse.com/
large-print-format-books

FIRST LARGE PRINT EDITION

Printed in the United States of America

10 9 8 7 6 5 4 3 2 1

This Large Print edition published in accord with the standards of the N.A.V.H.

CLASS ACT

1

Stone Barrington hipped his way out of a cab (the Bentley was being serviced) and found a discreet doorway with a polished brass number. He rang a bell, which was answered by a silken female voice. "How may I help you?" She made it sound more like a bordello than what he was looking for.

"Stone Barrington to see John Coulter."

"Please come in." A buzzer gently sounded.

Stone entered the doorway, which led him to another doorway, that led to a comfortably furnished sitting room—Chesterfield sofa, wing chairs, etcetera—which made the place seem more like an exclusive gentleman's club. A young woman in a Chanel suit sat behind a large mahogany desk. "Good morning," she said, identifying herself by her voice as the person Stone had heard on the intercom. "Mr. Barrington?"

"Yes."

"Will you follow me?"

That turned out to be an unexpected pleasure, as the suit was snug and its contents shapely. She led him to a door bearing a brass-plate placard: LARK was imprinted upon it. She knocked gently, but firmly. There was a muffled response, then she opened the door and stood back for Stone to enter first.

The room was akin to a junior suite in an upscale boutique hotel. Once the door had closed behind him, he found that even the hospital bed was made of mahogany, as was the rack beside it, from which a pair of IV bags were draped. The lighting was pleasant, without the usual glare, a cheerful conflagration burned in a gas fireplace and a silk dressing gown hung from a peg on the wall near the foot of the bed.

"Stone?" a man's voice asked. "Is that you? It hurts to open my eyes." The man was unidentifiable, because of a large bandage across the bridge of his nose.

"It is I, Jack. I hope you feel a good deal better than you look."

"They just gave me some morphine. It will kick in shortly, then I'll feel human again." Jack Coulter's voice was the well-modulated, upper-accented baritone Stone had expected.

"Ahhhh," Jack breathed.

"The morphine kicked in?"

"I'm probably going to become addicted before they let me out of here. Would you like a drink?"

"What, grain alcohol?"

"There's a bar in the cupboard over there." Jack waved a hand.

Stone opened the door and found a full wet bar—sink, ice machine, a row of Baccarat whiskey glasses, and a dozen choices of libation. He found a bottle of Knob Creek bourbon, filled a glass with ice, then filled that with bourbon. "I'm not offering you one, because I don't think you should mix booze and morphine," he said.

"I don't need it," Jack said contentedly. "Have a seat."

Stone pulled up a well-padded, burnished leather armchair and sank into it. Jack seemed to doze for a moment. Stone took the opportunity to reminisce about his first encounter with the man who had walked into his office, in his Turtle Bay townhouse, a few years back. He was maybe six-four, 250, wearing a dated suit that he could barely button. He had had a haircut that had been inflicted entirely with electric shears, and had been carrying a large suitcase and a smaller, non-matching duffel. He was frightening, until he spoke, in a voice much like the one he used now. He was also a good storyteller.

His name was John Fratelli, he said, and he had been a guest at an upstate hostelry called Sing Sing, until early that morning. He had spent the past twenty-three years there and had served all his time, without application for parole.

That explained the haircut, Stone thought, and the twenty-three years explained the suit. Stone inquired as to why he had not accepted parole. Fratelli explained that he had had an obligation to protect a fellow resident, who was smaller and weaker than he, and who had been in increasingly delicate health for the past three years. A few days earlier, he had died in his bed. His name was Eduardo Buono.

Fratelli's name meant nothing to Stone, but Buono's rang a loud bell. He had been the mastermind behind the heist of fifteen million dollars from a currency-handling operation at John F. Kennedy Airport, after which he had distributed half the take among a half dozen abettors, then vanished into the mists with the other seven and a half million, after instructing them not to spend a penny of the money for a year. They had, of course, paid off their bookies, were fitted with new wardrobes, and drove shiny new Cadillacs off dealers' lots—all this in the first two weeks after their score. When arrested and confronted with their misdeeds and the sentences they would probably draw, they had ratted out, as the expression goes, their benefactor, Eduardo Buono, who thereafter never said a word to anybody until he met John Fratelli, on the bus from Rikers Island to Ossining.

The two men had bonded on the drive up, to the point where Buono had confessed to his new friend that he was terrified of being raped in prison and sought his help in avoiding that fate. Fratelli's mien was imposing enough that few challenged him, and Buono had served his time virginally. Late in his life he gave Fratelli a reward for his fealty, the name and address of a New York City bank and the number of a large safe-deposit box and its key, which had resided for better than two decades in the orifice he had been so anxious to protect.

Fratelli said he had just come from the bank.

Stone had looked at the man's tatty luggage with new respect and discovered what appeared to be two bullet holes. Fratelli said that someone had gotten there ahead of him and had been waiting when he left the bank.

For the next hour or so, the two men had conducted a wide-ranging discussion, under the protection of attorney-client privilege, on the means of disappearing from New York City, arriving in a place where Fratelli could be more anonymous, change his identity, and make more secure banking arrangements. Stone had also directed him to Brooks Brothers, where he could find apparel more suitable to the current quarter of the century.

Stone had heard from Fratelli sporadically, piecing together his story from their chats over the years. Fratelli had lost weight, grown hair, opened an offshore account, and met a very nice woman and her family, who were people of means. A few months later Stone had attended their wedding, and they had settled down in Hillary Coulter's Fifth Avenue apartment. The next time Stone had seen them was at a large dinner party in that apartment, during which men with shotguns had entered and relieved all present of their jewelry. Jack Coulter had thought people from his past had done it, but that turned out not to be true.

"Stone," Jack said, waking from his reverie. "I expect you want to know how I got here."

"If you'd like to tell me, Jack."

"Michael O'Brien," he explained.

O'Brien had been among the Detectives investigating the robbery, and he thought he had recognized Coulter as Fratelli. Stone had disabused him of that notion, and they had heard no more about it, until now.

"Tell me how it happened," Stone said.

2

Jack Coulter said he had been walking up Lexington Avenue, alone. "I had just had a haircut and manicure at my regular barbershop, Nino's, in a hotel around the corner," he said. "I was shoved from behind. When I turned to look at the source of the aggravation, I caught a brief glimpse of O'Brien's face, then I was struck in the face by what I believe to have been a blackjack. The next thing I remember was my wife, Hillary, bending over me and saying that an ambulance was on the way."

"How did Hillary happen to be there?"

"She was walking down Lex in the opposite direction and saw a crowd of people hovering over someone, who turned out to be me. I passed out again and woke up in this hospital. Hillary knew the place, because she had a facelift here a couple of years ago. They specialize in facial work, and she wanted me to have the best possible nose man."

"I'm sure it will be fine, once you're healed," Stone said.

"The doctor says it will be better than fine. He worked from some old photos of me that Hillary had on her iPhone. He says people won't recognize me with my new nose."

"That sounds good. How long before it goes on display?"

"A couple of weeks or so," Jack said. "I'll have to wear a plastic cup over it for a while, so as not to frighten people. Right now, without the bandage, I've got two black eyes, and look like a raccoon."

"I look forward to meeting the new you."

"I thought, as long as I have to wear a disguise for a couple of weeks, I might as well find Detective Michael O'Brien and kill him."

"Whoa, there, Jack," Stone said. "That won't solve anything; you'd be in worse trouble than before. I take it O'Brien wants your seven million dollars."

"It's a lot more than that now. I invested wisely."

"I should consult you for stock tips," Stone said.

"I can introduce you to a friend from childhood who operates out of South Florida. If you've got a million to invest, he'll get you five percent a week."

"He must be one hell of a stockbroker," Stone said.

"He's a loan shark, who works for the biggest bookie in the state of Florida. The bookie feeds him a steady flow of borrowers."

"Well, that's interesting, but not for me. Do you think it's a secure means of investing?"

"Well, he doesn't know my new name or where I am. His organization sends couriers with cash to various offshore banks, then they wire my five percent to my offshore account."

"They have that account number?"

"There's one account number set up for deposits, and a different one for withdrawals."

"Suppose your, ah, lending friend or his boss should just decide to keep your million and not pay?"

"They know I can find them. Before I was incarcerated I had a mostly undeserved reputation for personal violence, mainly because of my appearance, which, you may remember, was more fearsome then."

"Fearsome it was," Stone said.

"I think it will be less so when I have healed."

"Then it might be a good idea to lie low until you do."

"We're going to spend a few weeks at Hillary's place in Northeast Harbor, Maine," Jack said. "We won't be going out."

"I think you know that I knew Michael O'Brien before his retirement from the NYPD," Stone said.

"I do."

"He was a very good Detective, and was noted in the squad for his perseverance. Once on a case he was like a dog with a bone—he never, never let go."

"Then I may have to revert to plan A," Jack said. "Don't worry. I won't shoot him down in the street. I know people who know people who would take care of it."

"Jack, are you looking for a free ticket back to Sing Sing?"

"Don't worry about me, Stone. Come to dinner when we get back. I'll introduce you to my new nose." Then Jack dozed off again.

Stone and his old NYPD partner, Dino Bacchetti, now the city's police commissioner, were dining at P. J. Clarke's, where the noise level covered their conversation. Since Dino was the only other person who knew about Jack Coulter's identity, with the possible exception of Michael O'Brien and anyone else he might have told, Stone could speak freely. He told Dino about the sudden alteration of Jack's appearance.

"It's ironic," Dino said, "that the only person

who is hunting down John Fratelli is the one responsible for making him unrecognizable."

"Let's hope," Stone said. "We haven't seen the results of the surgery yet."

"Responding to your request, I got a report on O'Brien's behavior just before and after his, ah, retirement from the NYPD."

"Oh, good. I take it the retirement wasn't entirely voluntary."

"It was explained to him that he had two choices: he could go to trial on charges of abetting the robbery at Jack Coulter's apartment, or he could turn in his papers and live out his life with a decent pension."

"You're satisfied that O'Brien is the guy who tipped the robbers to the gathering of all that expensive jewelry?"

"By a process of elimination, yes. I'm not sure we would win at trial, but we could indict him, and that would ruin him in the department."

"What information do you have on O'Brien's existence since he turned in his papers?"

"He's been doing rather well, except for the part about being a degenerate gambler."

"Where's he getting all the money he's losing?"

"His mother."

"I somehow thought he was from a fairly poor family."

"He was, until his father died and his mother

remarried, and rather well. She was the cashier at a good restaurant downtown. Her boss fell in love with her and, after she was widowed, they were married."

"How much of a gap between husband one and husband two?"

"Not much. And husband two was very well off when he died a couple of years later. She sold the restaurant to some of their employees and gave them a mortgage, so she has a fine income—at least, what she can keep out of Mike's hands."

"Has anybody explored the convenient death of husband one?"

"It has been suggested that she may have helped him along toward that goal, but there is insufficient evidence to charge her."

"I would imagine that her son could have been a great help to her in knocking him off, being a cop and all."

"We imagined that, too, but again, we couldn't prove it."

"Still that possibility might be something that could be dangled over O'Brien's head to keep him straight."

"Keeping him straight is important, I gather," Dino said.

"Suffice it to say that the Coulters are leaving town for a couple of weeks, until his new nose emerges. After that, he believes, he'll be harder to spot on Lexington Avenue."

"Good. Does that end the necessity of this conversation?"

"No. Jack has expressed an interest in removing O'Brien from the planet on a permanent basis."

"Then . . . Which one are we trying to protect?"

"Coulter, who, if he had his way, would endanger his personal freedom."

"You think Mike will forget about this while he's gone?"

"No. If you ever worked a case with O'Brien—"

"Several."

"Then you will recall his perseverance in pursuit of a suspect."

"Oh, yeah. Right."

"Also, if the reports you heard about his gambling habit are true, he is in perpetual need of money. And he may have worn out his welcome with his mother. I think he sees the downfall of Jack Coulter as the source of a windfall of funds."

"Well, there is the seven million Jack liberated from Buono's safe-deposit box, isn't there?"

"Jack says it's a lot more, now. A loan shark of his early acquaintance is sending him fifty Gs a week in interest on a million bucks Jack invested with him. And, as you know, Jack has been married to a very wealthy woman for some years now."

"All that makes him low-hanging fruit for O'Brien?"

"Obviously."

"And Jack is sure it was Michael?"

"Two things: First, a blackjack is a police weapon, albeit an illegal one in most circumstances. Second, Jack caught a glimpse of O'Brien immediately before he was struck."

"So," Dino said, "what is it you want—or rather, want me—to do?"

3

Stone settled into his desk chair and contemplated the stack of papers next to his keyboard.

His secretary, Joan, contemplated Stone. "Dino scanned and e-mailed that to you. I printed it out, since I know how you hate reading screens."

"That's thoughtful of you," Stone replied. "It would have been even more thoughtful of you if you had printed half the stack."

"Which half?" Joan asked.

"Oh, all right, I'll read it."

"It appears to be police files on one Michael Xavier O'Brien," Joan said. "A retired police officer."

"Have you read the whole thing?" Stone asked. "Because if you have, you can just give me the gist and save me a lot of time."

"Well, maybe not the **whole** thing," Joan said. "A lot of it, though."

"How much?" Stone asked.

Joan inserted a fingernail about three-quarters of the way down the stack. "About to here," she said.

"And you remember all of what you read?"

"Pretty much."

"Okay," Stone said, handing her the whole stack, "finish it, then brief me."

"Okay," Joan replied cheerfully. She picked up the stack and trotted back to her office.

Stone's phone buzzed. "Yes?"

"Dino, on one."

Stone pressed the button. "Good morning."

"Why?" Dino asked. "Aren't you reading the file?"

"Joan is reading it. She's already three-quarters through."

"I couldn't even print it that fast."

"I seem to remember that she took a speed-reading course a while back, but I haven't seen the results until now."

"She'll never be able to retain it long enough to pass it on to you."

"I heard that," Joan said over the speaker.

"You weren't supposed to," Stone said. "You were supposed to be reading the rest of the file."

"I've read the rest of the file," she said.

"I don't believe you."

"Ask me something about Michael X. O'Brien."

"How old is he?"

"Fifty."

"Where does he live?"

"In Brooklyn, in his mother's house."

"What was his mother's maiden name?"

"O'Brien."

"No, that was her married name."

"She married her third cousin, O'Brien. He got her the job at his brother's restaurant."

"And the brother's name was, of course, O'Brien."

"Correct."

"So her full name is . . ."

"Louise O'Brien O'Brien."

"And the name of the restaurant was . . . ?"

"O'Brien's."

"Of course, it was.

"Why did Mike retire?"

"At his own request. I'm surprised the department didn't request it. The guy is a real little shit."

"He was allowed to turn in his papers. His rabbi kept him safe," Dino said.

"No, he's Irish Catholic," Joan replied.

"She doesn't know what a rabbi is," Stone said.

"A rabbi," Dino said, "is like a mentor. If a cop has a good enough rabbi, he's more likely to be kept out of trouble."

"Who was his rabbi?" Stone asked.

"Captain James P. Moran," Dino replied. "If

you'd had Moran as a rabbi, you'd be in my job by now."

"No rabbi is that good."

"What I don't understand," Joan said, "is **why** he had such a great rabbi. Why did the guy take him on and keep him out of trouble for, what, thirty years since the academy?"

"I'll tell you," Dino said. "Moran was **schtupping** O'Brien's mother for all that time."

"How's your Yiddish, Joan?" Stone asked.

"Good enough to cover **schtupping**."

"Does that explain everything?"

"They were next-door neighbors in Brooklyn Heights," Dino said.

"Heights?" Stone asked. "How could a widow afford that neighborhood?"

"By marrying her boss," Dino replied. "She was the bookkeeper for a very good restaurant. And it's my bet she was **schtupping** the boss, too, because he married her, then had the good grace to die a couple of years later. She inherited the restaurant, then sold it to the employees and now lives the life of a rich widow, which is how O'Brien affords his relationship with the ponies."

"What sort of gambler is he?" Stone asked.

"Degenerate," Dino replied.

"It doesn't say that in his file," Joan pointed out.

"That's why it pays to have a rabbi who's **schtupping** his mother," Dino said. "Moran did a little laundering where O'Brien's file is concerned."

"In that case," Joan said, "all the good stuff is missing from his file."

"You might say that," Dino said.

"Why don't you fill us in with what you know, Dino?" Stone asked. "It will save Joan a lot of reading."

"I'm done reading," Joan said.

"Speak, Dino."

"All right, he's a degenerate gambler, which means he's eternally in search of a rigged horse race, so he can make a killing and pay off his bookie. Except his mother always pays off his bookie."

"She's an indulgent sort, isn't she?" Stone said.

"I'll say she is," Joan cut in. "She indulged her boss and the rabbi, too. She must have been a looker."

"I saw her once, years ago," Dino said. "She had the kind of breasts that couldn't be bought, in those days."

"Okay," Joan said. "I think I've heard enough about the widow O'Brien. Let me know if there's anything else you need to know about her son." She hung up.

"Is she gone?" Dino asked.

"Yeah."

"Well, just between you and me, the widow O'Brien had more going for her than great tits;

she had a very fine ass, too. I met her at a party that Moran threw, and she was the talk of the station house for months. She was even pretty, in that Irish lass sort of way—you know, the creamy skin."

"I'm happy for her," Stone said.

"We never knew why O'Brien was so ugly."

"And let's not start guessing," Stone said.

"Oh, that could be it. She could have been **schtupping** somebody less handsome than her husband or Moran."

"Let me know when you find out," Stone said, and hung up.

4

Jack Coulter woke up as his hospital bed began moving to the sitting position.

"The doctor wants to have a look at you," his nurse said.

Jack took a couple of deep breaths and tried opening his eyes wide. They didn't work all that well.

The doctor stood at the foot of the bed. "All right," he said, "curtain up."

The nurse removed the plastic nose guard, then the doctor, using tweezers, carefully pulled away the bandage. "Ahh," he said.

"Ahh good, or ahh bad?" Jack asked.

"We only do good around here," the doctor replied. "It looks perfect. You'll be out of here in a day or two, suitably masked, of course. Your raccoonness should have subsided by then, and you'll only have the surgical bruising to deal with."

"How do I deal with surgical bruising?" Jack asked.

"By not getting punched in the nose, or bumping into things. All you have to do is be careful. I understand you'll be traveling this week. When you do, you should wear a clear face guard, in case of accidents."

"How's my nose going to look when I'm healed?"

"You remember when you went to the movies as a kid and people like Tyrone Power and Errol Flynn were starring?"

"Sure."

"Like that."

"I guess I can live with that."

"I guess you'll have to," the doctor replied. "New bandage and cup," he said to the nurse. "Good morning, Mr. Coulter." He turned and left the room.

"You were lucky," the nurse said, beginning her work.

"How's that?"

"You got the best nose man in New York. All those friends of yours who have perfect noses? They went to him, too."

"That's encouraging."

"But don't tell them I told you so."

* * *

Mickey O'Brien sat in a reclining chair in the living room of his apartment in the basement of his mother's Brooklyn Heights townhouse and watched Bridal Veil turn the corner into the home stretch, half a length ahead of the nearest competition. Mickey had ten grand on her nose, which he had been promised would reach the finish line first, even if they had to shoot another horse. He had odds of twelve to one, and this win was going to make everybody he owed well again. He took a deep breath and began to let it out slowly. Then the impossible happened.

The filly seemed to trip over something with her left forefoot, but there was nothing there to trip over. Her right leg went rigid in a wild attempt to stop, then the horse on her rump collided with her, and they both went down, causing a series of catastrophes akin to an interstate car crash in thick fog. The horse who had been half a length behind crossed the line unpursued.

Mickey might as well have taken an arrow in the chest. He started to get to his feet, then fell back into the recliner. His mother's entrance coincided with that moment.

"Ohmigod, now what?" she asked. "I know that look," she said accusingly, "it happens when you lose and lose big."

"Mom," Mickey said weakly, throwing up an arm as if to stop her progress. "Don't start, not now!"

"I'm not starting," Louise O'Brien said firmly, "I'm finished, done with your sickness. You will not see another dime from me that will go to some sorry bookie somewhere!"

Mickey clutched himself and turned onto his side, away from the slings and spears that were being delivered from her direction.

"You get out of this house right now!" she yelled. "And don't you darken my door between the hours of nine AM and midnight. Why don't you go get a nice bouncer's job in some disco somewhere, like a respectable ex-cop. Bring home a paycheck!"

"Mom, I don't need a paycheck. I've got a pension! And a good one!"

"And every dime of it ends up in your bookie's pocket!" She was screaming now. "You might as well have your pension on auto-deposit to that bookie's pocket!"

"Stop, stop, please. I just saw my horse—running at twelve to one at full speed, collapse on the home stretch." He waved at the big TV. "Just look at that mess!"

Louise did look, and it was a mess, she would give him that. "Get out! Take your gun and go shoot that horse! Put him out of his misery!"

"It's a filly."

"I don't give a good goddamn what it is!"

"They're shooting her now," Mickey said, pointing. A group had gathered around the filly, and somebody was holding a tarp between her and the camera, then a forklift moved onto the track, and she was taken away.

Mickey was crying real tears now. "Poor goddamned baby!" he cried, watching the lump under the tarp be driven through a gate.

Louise grabbed the coal shovel from the fireplace set and whacked her son on the shoulder with it. He got his jacket on and fled the premises.

"Your key won't work before midnight!" Louise yelled after him. "I'll fix that!"

Mickey flagged a cab and, before he could think, nearly gave it the address of his favorite bar. But if he went there, he would be sent home with broken legs, and his mother would do the rest.

"P. J. Clarke's," he said to the driver. His crowd didn't drink there. They didn't like the class of people it drew. They dressed too well and smelled too good, they drank twelve-year-old Scotch, and they didn't fuck people like them.

Mickey's worst fears were realized when he got inside the crowded bar and immediately came face-to-face with the police commissioner of New York City and that snotty friend of his, Barrington.

"Look who's here!" Dino cried gleefully. "We don't even have to go look for him! Come on in, Mickey, and buy us a drink!"

Mickey got out the door quickly and sprinted up Third Avenue; he knew not where, just out of there. He wished he could get out of his life, too.

5

Jack Coulter was wakened by his nurse on the day of his discharge. She shaved him, changed his bandage, and set out his clothes, which had been laundered, dry-cleaned, and pressed, and his shoes polished. She helped him dress and get seated in a wheelchair, then a breakfast cart and table was wheeled in and he had a sumptuous breakfast.

When he was done, the nurse took away the cart, set his trench coat and hat in his lap, and pushed his wheelchair to the porte cochere, where his Bentley awaited. He said goodbye to the nurse and gave her an envelope of hundreds to be shared as she saw fit, then he gave his coat and hat to the driver and got into the rear seat beside Hillary.

"Well, you look fresh and almost new," she said, kissing him carefully, to avoid a nose bump.

"Never better," Jack said.

They were driven to Teterboro and thence to Jet Aviation, where a Citation CJ3 awaited them, one owned by the office supply company now owned by Hillary, and one of two available for their use. Minutes later, they were climbing through clouds, then, finally, in clear blue skies. Jack dozed off.

An hour later, Jack awoke when he felt the landing gear come down and five minutes after that they coasted to a stop at Columbia Aviation at Bar Harbor Airport, where they and their luggage were loaded into a Range Rover and driven to the charming village of Northeast Harbor, where they occupied a charming house overlooking the charming harbor. Jack settled into an armchair with a view and allowed the **New York Times** to be placed in his hands. He was brought a cup of tea, then Hillary settled into a chair opposite him and opened the island newspaper.

"Was there anything in the New York papers about my, ah, mishap?" he asked.

"Nothing that could identify you," she replied. "You know, the **Post** said something like, 'Man mugged on Lex, assailant sought.'"

"No photographs?"

"Oh, some tourist got a snap of you being loaded into the ambulance, then shopped it to the **Post**. You were unidentifiable."

"Has anyone been sniffing around our building?"

"Nothing the deskman couldn't handle."

"I expect O'Brien will be asking."

"Let him ask."

Mickey O'Brien flashed his gold badge at the doorman and entered the building without being stopped. He got only as far as the desk, where he flashed it again.

"Hello, O'Brien," the deskman said. "Don't they make you turn in your badge when you retire?"

"Usually," O'Brien said, "but not Detectives. I need to see Jack Coulter."

"**Mister** Coulter is not at home."

"Yeah, I know what that means."

"He left the city this morning."

"For where?"

"His summer home."

"And where's that?"

"Now, that's not a question you expect to have answered, is it?"

"I expect to have **all** my questions answered."

"Dream on, Mickey. We all know what you did, and if you walk in here again, I'll have Internal Affairs on your back, and you know how they cling."

"Fuck you," O'Brien said, but left. He crossed

Fifth Avenue, and found a bench against the Central Park wall with a view of the building. Now, where would a gent of Coulter's station have a summer house? Hamptons? Nah, too flash. Cape Cod? Maybe that or the Vineyard or Nantucket. He needed to narrow the range. As he thought about it, a blue Bentley with Florida plates turned the corner and entered the building's garage.

Florida plates? Jack had a place in Palm Beach, didn't he? He trotted across the street and into the garage. The Bentley was parked near the entrance, and Mickey checked the plate. It was in a dealer's frame with a West Palm address, and he jotted down the license number, then trotted back to his bench and got out his phone. He got himself connected to the West Palm Beach police and gave them another Detective's name, at the 19th Precinct.

"What can we do for you, Chief?" the cop asked.

"I need a little info on a man named Jack Coulter, lives part time in P.B., drives a Bentley from the local dealer." He spelled Coulter for the man.

"Okay, let's see. What d'ya know? Man had a couple parking tickets on Worth Avenue."

"Where does he live?"

"Local address at a big hotel called the Breakers."

"Any other address?"

"One on Fifth Avenue, New York City, one in Northeast Harbor, Maine, on Harborside Road. That's it."

"That's all I need," O'Brien said and hung up. Maine! Why didn't he think of that? He went to the maps on his iPhone and looked up the address. Harborside Road was fairly short, and there was an airport less than ten miles away: Bar Harbor Airport.

He called a travel agent. He could get to Northeast Harbor by flying to Boston and changing for Bar Harbor, where he could rent a car. He looked at his watch: a little late in the day. He made a reservation for tomorrow, then started looking for a bar where he wouldn't stand out too much.

Late in the evening, Mickey got out of a cab into pouring rain and ran for the door to his basement apartment. He stuck in his key, but it wouldn't turn in any direction. Befuddled, he searched his brain for some reason. Then he remembered what his mother had screamed at him before he left the house. The locksmith had done his work and replaced the old lock with one set to unlock on a timer.

He checked his wristwatch for the time, but couldn't see it. The bulb under the main staircase had burned out. He walked around trying to find a ray of light to reveal his watch, then Nature obliged with a quick bolt of lightning. Eleven-forty, it read, so he was required to shelter under the stairs for another twenty minutes before his key would work.

It didn't work then, either, but finally, after another three minutes the key opened the door. He left his sodden clothing in a pile by the front door and got into a hot shower, to warm his bones. That accomplished, he set up a clothesline in the kitchen and hung his clothes there to drip dry, then got into a bed that eventually became warm.

6

Mickey O'Brien got himself slowly together the next morning, then wrote his mother a note and stuck it on the door.

> **Mom, I've got to go out of town on business today, but I should be back by around six p.m. Book us a dinner table somewhere you love, and it's on me! The day holds promise!**
> **Your loving son,**
> **Michael**

Jack Coulter was awakened by a warm hand on his thigh, which moved further.

"Is this working yet?" Hillary asked.

Somewhat to his surprise, it was, and the two

enjoyed a romp in the hay that was up to pre-blackjack standards.

After a little tidy-up of the bed, Hillary rang, and a few minutes later the housekeeper, Mae, pushed in a cart loaded with breakfast and served them in bed.

"Any thoughts on what to do today?" Hillary asked.

"I don't know, how about a cruise up the sound, aboard **Maine Belle**?" Jack replied. "The weather is glorious."

"Oh, yes; we'll have lunch. I'll ring up the captain and give him his instructions. Twelve o'clock? That will give the cook time to shop."

"Perfect."

Jack got himself into his yacht club Brenton Reef red trousers, a white shirt, and a club necktie, then donned a blue blazer and threw a sweater around his shoulders, in case the wind got up.

Hillary installed a fresh bandage and a nose guard.

Mickey made his early-morning flight to Boston in a rush, then sat in the airport there for hours, waiting for them to do something to the puddle jumper that was the only way to Bar Harbor. He read the papers and thought about the ponies but didn't do anything about them, then formulated a plan for his eventual arrival.

Upon landing, he went to the rental car booth in the tiny terminal and asked for something small. All they had was a Chevy Suburban, a domestic tank, but they gave him a lower rate. They gave him a map, too, which included an inset of Northeast Harbor.

He crossed an almost unnoticeable bridge to Mount Desert Island, and made his way to Northeast Harbor. His approach was right down Harborside Road, where there were a couple of dozen houses but no way to identify Jack Coulter's. Then he spotted a green Range Rover pulling out of a driveway ahead of him and thought, What the hell, how many of those could there be around at this time of year? Labor Day had been a couple of weeks ago, and the village was deserted.

Mickey hung back from the Range Rover, which was driven by a woman with a man at her side. He followed them down to the harbor marina, where they parked and walked down the dock to a handsome motor yacht from the twenties or thirties, Mickey thought. The man was big enough to be John Fratelli. He saw them walk up the gangplank, then, a moment later, two crew cast off, and the yacht moved gracefully down the harbor. He noted the name on her stern, **Maine Belle.**

Mickey looked around for a boat to rent or steal but saw nothing. Most of the berths were empty. He noticed a chart posted on a bulletin board and tried to guess where the yacht might go. As he looked up, she was leaving the harbor and turning right. A light breeze had come up, and his guess was that she would stay in sheltered waters. He liked the look of a body of water called Somes Sound and thought that looked perfect for a day cruise. He got into the car and switched on the GPS navigator as he drove up to the main street. Then he saw a shop with a sign in the window: SPORTING GOODS, FISHING AND HUNTING GEAR. He parked and got out. All he had on him was his 9mm handgun; he needed more range.

Mickey walked into the shop and had a look around. There was a rack of used rifles at the rear, and he headed there.

"Something I can do for you?" an elderly man behind the counter said.

"Oh, maybe something light, with a scope. Something good for varmits." He looked over the weapons in the rack and found a .30-caliber military carbine, probably of World War II vintage.

"That's a great old weapon," the shopkeeper said.

"Will it take a scope?"

"Sure it will. And I can install it. Mind you, the scope costs more than the rifle. I can mount it in half an hour," he added.

"How about a silencer?" Mickey asked.

"Sure, those are legal these days. I can do the threads for that, too."

They haggled a bit, then agreed on a price. "If you'll throw in a box of ammo," Mickey said. "I'll take a walk while you work."

"Turn over that sign on the door so it reads CLOSED," the man said. "That'll make things go faster."

Mickey did so, then stepped into the street.

A row of shops and galleries ran down the street, some of them with empty windows. He found an open restaurant called the Colonel and had a sandwich, then he walked back to the sporting goods shop.

The proprietor was screwing in the silencer. "Pretty neat, huh?"

"Pretty neat," Mickey replied. "Got a canvas case for it?"

The man produced one. Mickey inspected the rifle, then slipped it into the case. He paid the man in cash, from his emergency stash, for when a great long shot came along, and left the shop. He tucked the rifle into the front passenger seat and followed his GPS map to a road called Sargeant Drive, which ran up the eastern side of Somes Sound. He pulled over about halfway up the sound, next to a boulder and a cutback pine tree, then got out. He looked up and down the sound and saw nothing, not so much as a sailing dinghy. He was expressing disgust with his guess of the yacht's routing when it hove into sight from behind a boulder, perhaps half a mile away.

Mickey went to the Suburban, got out the rifle case, unzipped it, and shook out the weapon. He popped the magazine and began loading the cartridges. There was an extra magazine, but he reckoned he wouldn't need that. The boat was chugging up the sound at, maybe, six or seven knots. He walked to the boulder by the pine tree and settled the rifle into a notch along the top. He noted that the wind was shifting to the east and freshening, and its skipper cheated it into the shore, where the wind was lighter.

Mickey began to sight in on his target.

7

Mickey trained his sights on the spot where the skipper would drive the boat. He could see the man through the windshield, talking to a young woman. He swung his aim to the right and drew a bead on a lobster pot buoy, then squeezed off a round. He was pleased with how quiet the rifle was with the silencer, and he saw the bullet splash a foot ahead of the buoy.

The wind came up a bit more, and Mickey adjusted his sights: he hit the pot squarely, and at that moment, the helmsman cut back the power and slowed the boat. He said something to the woman, and she began moving aft. He hoped they hadn't seen the hit on the buoy.

Now he could see the couple, who were sitting all the way aft, on a sofa that curved around the stern, making for an easy pick-off. Then the woman came onto the afterdeck, holding blankets in her arms. The man waved her off, then escorted his wife off the afterdeck and into the main cabin. They had gotten chilly, it seemed. Shit.

Now his shot was harder to make. The sun reflected off the glass windows of the main cabin, distorting the images of whoever was inside. He could see movement, but he couldn't be sure which person was Fratelli or his wife or a crew member. Then, for just a moment, the sun's angle changed, and he had a clear view of the man.

He resighted, moving the crosshairs to the center of the man's chest, then the sight picture went blank. He lifted his head from the stock of the rifle and looked at the yacht. The crew woman had pulled down a shade in the cabin, and she pulled down another as he watched. He had no picture and no shot.

Mickey looked up and down the sound wondering where they would turn back for the trip down the sound. Wherever it was, he figured, he would have no shot. Oh, well. He removed the magazine and racked the slide, ejecting the round in the chamber, then he looked at his watch. It was one o'clock, and that was the time his flight left. He heard a noise and saw the puddle jumper clear the mountain across the sound, then turn to the south. It was the only flight for the rest of the day. How could he have gotten it so wrong?

He got into the car and pulled out his cell

phone, got a signal, and did a search for aircraft charters. He found a flight school at Bar Harbor Airport that also advertised charters. He called the number and got the manager on the line.

"What can I do you for?" a man with a Mainer accent said.

"Have you got something to charter that can fly me to Teterboro, New Jersey?"

"When?"

"Right away."

"Just a minute." There were paper-shuffling noises. "I've got a Baron."

"What's a Baron?"

"A twin-engine Beechcraft, an excellent airplane. I'd suggest flying to Caldwell, New Jersey, about ten miles west of Teterboro. Nice little airport there and our route would keep us out of all the corporate stuff landing and taking off at Teterboro."

"How long a flight?"

"About two, two and a half hours. It's quite a comfortable airplane. How many people?"

"Just me."

"Any luggage?"

"Just a rifle case."

"As long as I hold on to the ammo." He offered a price, they haggled, then made the deal.

"I'll be there in about fifteen, twenty minutes," Mickey said. "I have to turn in my rental car at the terminal."

"I'll taxi around and wait for you there. My tail number is November 123 Tango Foxtrot."

"See you then." Mickey started the car and turned it around. He saw the motor yacht making its turn, too, heading back down the sound. He had been right; he wouldn't have had a shot. He drove back to the airport, handed in the car, then walked out to the ramp, where a twin had just shut down its engines. The tail number was the right one.

He walked out, shook the pilot's hand, and, at his invitation, stowed the rifle in the forward luggage compartment, and the ammo with it.

The pilot did a brief walk-around, then Mickey hopped into the rear compartment and made himself comfortable. Ten minutes later, they were lifting off.

The winds were favorable at their altitude, and they made it in a little more than two hours. The pilot had called ahead for a car and driver.

It was after five, and in rush-hour traffic, the drive to Brooklyn took almost as long as the flight from Maine. He called his mother.

"Where are you, Mickey? Are you going to make dinner?"

"I'm in a car, on the way home. What time is our table?"

"Eight o'clock, at Peter Luger."

The best steak house in the city, and one of the most expensive. Dinner was going to be upwards of two hundred dollars.

"Great! Love the place. I need to change clothes. Unlock the door, will you?"

"Already done."

"See you at seven-forty-five, out front." He hung up. "You want to drive us to dinner?" he asked the driver.

"Sure, but I'll have to drop you. I've got another booking at eight-thirty."

"Done." Mickey settled back in the seat and explored his options. There weren't many.

8

Stone was wrapping up his day when Joan buzzed. "Will you accept a call from the president of the United States?" she asked.

"Oh, all right."

"I knew you'd be excited."

There was a click. "Stone?" Holly said brightly.

"One and the same. Where are you?"

"In New York, as it happens. Dinner tonight? I'm sorry I couldn't give you more notice, but I was locked into the UN all day."

"You mean dine out in public, like in a restaurant?"

"Sort of. I've booked a private dining room at Peter Luger. I'm dying for a steak."

"Is there a bed in that room?"

"I've got that all worked out," she said. "You're sleeping at the Carlyle, so bring a change of socks."

"Will do."

"Eightish," she said. "We'll arrive in separate cars." She hung up.

Stone hung up, too. The thing with the cars was always a problem. If they arrived anywhere together, the paparazzi were waiting for them when they left. On departure, Holly went first, taking the crowd with her, so Stone could get to his car unmolested.

When Mickey got home he asked the driver to wait and take them to the restaurant. His key worked. He showered, dressed in his best suit, and was waiting for Louise at the front door, having robbed his secret stash of some more money.

At the restaurant they were seated at her favorite table; a Rob Roy was brought for her and a single malt Scotch for him.

"So," she said, "how was your business day?"

"It went well. I had to fly to Maine to see a client."

"How much did that cost?"

"He paid. The yield here could be great."

"How soon?"

"A week or two."

"A toast to income," Louise said, raising her glass.

"I'm all for that," Mickey said, sipping his

Scotch. He ordered the porterhouse for two, and they had another drink.

"Trying to soften me up?" she asked.

"Trying to relax you. You deserve it."

"God knows I do."

Stone got to the restaurant first and was shown to the private room. As the door closed, he caught a glimpse of the restaurant floor and Michael O'Brien seated across from an older, attractive woman. That must be the mother, he thought.

Holly arrived and closed the door on the Secret Service agent behind her.

They enjoyed more than a momentary kiss.

"I suppose we could just clear the table and do it here," she said.

"I like a softer bed," Stone said, holding her chair for her. A waiter arrived with an icy martini and a Knob Creek on the rocks.

"To escape," Holly said, toasting.

"I'll drink to that."

"I thought I was going to get stuck with a bunch of diplomats," she said, "but I weaseled out of it."

They had finished their porterhouse when Louise removed an envelope from her bosom. "I have a little surprise for you," she said. "Open it later."

Mickey thought of excusing himself to the men's room and opening it there, but he resisted and tucked it away. He didn't want to annoy her.

"Oh, go ahead," she said.

He opened the envelope and removed a check for what he at first thought to be twenty thousand dollars, but he knew that was too much for a gift. Then he looked again. "Two million dollars?" he blurted.

"I sold some stock you were going to inherit anyway," Louise said. "But I want it understood what it's for."

"I'm flabbergasted," he said, reading the number again.

"First, you pay off your bookie. I want your promise that you will give up gambling, cold turkey. Otherwise, you'll never have a thing. Then I want you to buy a nice, little apartment."

"I like my present apartment," he said.

"Well, you can sit around there for the next forty years, waiting for me to die, I guess. I had in mind something you could move a wife into."

"First, I have to find a wife," he said.

She raised her glass. "To a better wife, next time."

"I'll drink to that."

Now Mickey excused himself to use the men's room. He got out his phone and made the call while standing at the urinal.

"It's Mickey. Gimme Al."

"Al don't want to speak to you. He just wants to know when."

"Tomorrow morning at ten, at my bank. He knows where that is. He gets paid then." He heard a keyboard clicking.

"It'll be eighteen-five with the vig."

"Done." He hung up, zipped his fly, turned around, and ran slap into Stone Barrington. "What are **you** doing here."

"Having dinner, like a normal human being," Stone replied, moving past him to occupy the urinal. "What's your excuse?"

"I'm taking my mother to dinner."

"Did you bring your blackjack?" Stone asked.

"What are you talking about?" Mickey sputtered.

"Every worn-out cop has one. If it ever touches a client of mine again, I'll deal with you myself. I have a blackjack, too."

"Oh, fuck off!" Mickey shouted, exiting the men's room.

"I intend to," Stone said to himself, adjusting his clothing. He went to rejoin Holly.

Later, in bed at the Carlyle, they made up for lost time.

9

Jack Coulter had seen the man behind the boulder and the barrel pointed his way. He had had the blinds drawn, and they had moved to the sitting room of their suite below. "I feel like a nap," he said to Hillary.

"I'll watch," she said, taking her book with her.

Belowdecks, he stretched out on their bed, while Hillary read before the little gas fire in their sitting room. Jack stared at the ceiling, unable to nod off. He had thought that, by this time, he would have faded so deep into the background of the upper class of New York, Palm Beach, and Northeast Harbor that he would never have been noticed. Then came Michael O'Brien, almost out of the woodwork.

He and Hillary had given a rather grand dinner party in their Fifth Avenue apartment when, before they could sit down, men in black hoods with shotguns had walked into the penthouse and robbed their dinner guests, one by one, taking their jewelry and cash, a big haul.

Stone Barrington had been a guest, sitting on the terrace, when he heard the racking of shotgun pumps. He had taken his date's jewelry and put it into a pocket, then called 911. The cops had been a little slow, and when they had burst in, weapons drawn, Michel O'Brien was among them, and the robbers were not. Jack hadn't thought O'Brien was involved, but then Michael caught his eye and winked at him. He had recognized Jack, in spite of his older, slimmer, and better-dressed self. From then on Jack hadn't slept as well, but he still had not been ready for the attack on Lexington Avenue.

Jack finally began to nod off. He knew now that he would have to become the aggressor, and they would have to get out of Maine at once. He drifted away.

At dinner at the Maine house that night Hillary took note that Jack personally locked all the doors and windows before sitting down.

"I read the weather reports in the **Times** today," she said, "and it's sunny and in the upper seventies in Palm Beach."

"Oh, really? Sounds perfect. It's a little dead here, what with all the summer people gone."

"You're looking quite good without the mask now. A touch of makeup, and you'd be a new man."

"Would you like to nip down to Palm Beach for a few days, then? Until I'm completely recovered?"

"I would enjoy that."

Over brandy after dinner, Jack found his cell phone and alerted their captain about their new flight plans.

The following morning the Coulters boarded their airplane and flew south.

Along the way, with Hillary sleeping, Jack moved to the rear of the airplane and picked up the satphone, tapping in the number.

"The Barrington Practice," said the woman who answered.

"It's Jack Coulter, for Mr. Barrington."

"Of course."

"Jack? It's good to hear from you. How are you coming along?"

"Almost there, Stone. Another week, perhaps."

"Where are you?"

"Flying south from Maine. We had an unfortunate encounter there, with our mutual acquaintance."

"What came of it?"

"Nothing, as it happened. He was lying in wait

for us along the shore of Somes Sound as we were cruising; he was armed with a rifle with a scope. Fortunately, I saw him, and we took evasive action. Now we're on our way to Palm Beach. I'll complete my recovery there."

"Good idea."

"Stone, I've taken all of this I can. Something must be done."

"Careful, Jack."

"I wondered if you knew someone who might discretely help."

"Jack, I'm not in that business. Anyway, you are probably in a better position to know such a person than I."

"I hate to return to the past."

"I understand, but I can't be a part of it."

"You're a wise man, Stone," Jack said, "and I'm sure you're right. Thank you for listening."

"Anytime, Jack. My best to Hillary." They both hung up.

Stone thought about it for a while, then called Bob Cantor, a jack-of-all-trades ex-cop and part-time private investigator.

"How are you, Stone?" Cantor asked.

"Good, but I have an acquaintance who isn't."

"Tell me about it."

"You remember a cop called Michael O'Brien? Mickey?"

"Who could forget him?"

"My acquaintance would like to."

"What does your acquaintance have in mind?" Cantor asked cautiously.

"Nothing drastic, but I want to know where Mickey is, every hour of the day. Can you put together a surveillance team?"

"Where does he live?"

"Brooklyn Heights, in his mother's basement." Stone gave him the address.

"Anything else you can tell me?"

"He was in Maine yesterday, looking for my acquaintance, and fortunately, didn't find him. He was at Peter Luger last night, treating his mother, though with what money I don't know. He's reportedly a gambler, and not a good one."

"Sounds like every mother's dream. Does he have any income?"

"A full pension from the NYPD. He's trying to screw my acquaintance out of millions."

"Sounds like he has something on your acquaintance."

"He does, but that's not relevant."

"It seems pretty relevant to your acquaintance, and to Mickey, too."

"True, but you don't need to know about that. If it becomes relevant, I'll tell you."

"Has Mickey threatened him?"

"He slugged him in the face with a blackjack on Lexington Avenue a week or so ago."

"I'd consider that a threat. Where does your acquaintance reside?"

"Fifth Avenue in the low sixties," Stone said. "If you see O'Brien around there, disturb him, but watch out for the blackjack."

"I'll get a couple of guys on him," Cantor said.

"No gorillas. I don't want Mickey to spot them and become overcautious."

"Got it. I'll be in touch."

They both hung up.

10

Mickey woke early the next morning, had some breakfast, showered, shaved, and put on his good suit and a tie. He dusted off his briefcase and brought that, too. He was at his bank at opening time and asked to see the manager, Henry Solomon. He was the guy who called when Mickey was overdrawn.

"Good morning, Michael," Solomon said. "What can I do for you?"

"I want to make a deposit," Mickey replied.

"Any teller can help you with that."

"Not this one. I also want to make a withdrawal." He placed the check on the desk.

"I see," the man said, his eyes widening slightly. "Your mother transferred some cash from her investment account yesterday."

"And I want thirty thousand dollars in cash back."

"Please wait a moment." Solomon took the check and went into his private office.

Mickey wasn't surprised. The man was calling his mother. Brooklyn Heights was like a small town; lots of people knew each other.

Soloman returned and sat down. He took out his pen, initialed a corner of the check, and handed it to Mickey. "There you are. Take it to teller number one."

Mickey shook the man's hand got a deposit slip from one of the tables, filled it out, and walked to the window. There was one customer ahead of him, and he used the time for a little discreet ogling of the teller, a small brunette who had paid little attention to him in the past. He moved to the window. "Hi, Geraldine, I want to make a deposit."

"Of course, Mr. O'Brien," she said, looking at the check. Her eyes widened more than her manager's had.

"It's **Detective** O'Brien, recently retired from the NYPD, but you can call me Mickey. I'd like thirty thousand in hundreds back, and a bank envelope."

She counted out the money twice, and he handed her back a hundred. "May I have two fifties, please?"

She took the hundred and gave him the fifties. He counted out $18,500 and tucked it into the envelope. "A charitable contribution," he said, tucking the rest into his pocket.

"Any time we can help, Mickey," she said.

"You could help by having dinner with me tomorrow night," he said. "Someplace nice."

"I'd love to." She scribbled her number on a bank card and handed it to him. "Let me know what time and where."

"Certainly." He walked to the front door and outside. His bookie, Tiny Blanco, a three-hundred-pounder, was waiting. "You better have it, Mick," he said. "Eighteen big ones, plus fifty."

Mickey slapped the envelope onto Tiny's chest. "Count it," he said. "And I want a receipt."

Tiny riffled through the money without taking it from the envelope. "We don't put nothing on paper," he said. "My word is good."

"Good enough for me, Tiny, and don't come looking for more."

"You want me to up your limit?"

"Nah, I'm giving up gambling. You took your last bet from me."

"Mick, don't be that way."

"Bye-bye, Tiny," he said, and walked away. Through a reflection in a shop window, he saw a car pull up and take Tiny away. That had been satisfying. He wondered what else he could do that morning that would be satisfying.

Mickey was stopped in his tracks by a display

of houses and apartments in the window of a real estate agency. A woman at a desk barely looked up at him. "May I help you?"

"You may sell me an apartment, if you're good enough at it."

She regarded his suit for a moment, then stood and offered her hand. "I'm Marjorie Twist," she said. "Call me Marge."

"I'm Detective Michael O'Brien, NYPD, recently retired. Call me Mickey." He shook the hand.

She indicated a seat at a round table in the middle of the room. "Let's have a look at some photographs," she said. "What did you have in mind?"

"Living room, dining area, kitchen, two bedrooms with baths, and a study, where I can think."

"In this neighborhood?"

"Yes."

"You're talking three-quarters of a million or more," she said.

"Okay."

She brought out a fat three-ring binder of photographs. "Have a look through these, and mark anything that interests you."

Mickey began leafing through the book, stopping to read the description of a place if he liked the look of it, then placing strips of paper to mark them. "I'm interested in these three," he said.

She looked quickly at the three and noted the addresses, then went to a key safe, unlocked it, and extracted three clumps of keys. “Then we’re off,” she said.

He looked at the first two, each of which had problems—one was too close to a busy street; another had no trees on the block. Then he saw the third. It was exactly what he had described to her. It was the first two floors of a townhouse, and there was a garage and garden out back. “Who lives upstairs?” he asked.

“All three apartments have been renovated,” she said, “and the upper two will be let.”

“What are they asking for the duplex?” he asked.

“Eight hundred thousand.”

“And a selling price for the other two?”

“Two hundred fifty thousand each. They’ll bring very nice rents and only went on the market today.”

“I’ll offer a million for all three.”

“I can write it up, but honestly, I don’t think it will fly.”

“The owner has a lot of bills to pay for the renovation and new appliances. He could use the cash.”

“Shall I tell you what I think he would grab at?”

“Sure.”

“A million and a half. And I think that’s a fair price.”

"All right, I'll offer a million and a quarter, but I won't pay more. It's take it or leave it. All cash at closing, and we can close as soon as he's done with any finishing work."

She opened her briefcase and set it on a kitchen counter. "I'll write up the offer." She filled out a form and showed him where to sign it. He did. "And I'll need a hundred and fifty thousand for earnest money." He wrote a check.

"Excuse me, I'll make a call."

She went into another room, where he could barely hear her voice, and talked rapidly for five minutes, then returned. "You've bought yourself a very nice property, Mickey." She shook his hand. "Do you have a car?"

"I'm going to buy one."

She handed him a key. "This is for the garage. You can use it immediately. I'll want it back, if the sale doesn't close."

"Okay."

"Can I buy you a celebratory lunch?"

"Sure, you can," Mick said. He felt warm all over.

11

Bob Cantor flopped down in the chair next to Stone's desk. "What have you got?" Stone asked.

"This could be good for your client."

"How's that?"

"Mickey O'Brien hit it big," Cantor said. "Probably a fixed race."

"How big?"

"Well, he paid a visit to his bank this morning and made a deposit and got cash back, a transaction that required the approval of the manager; that indicates a substantial sum. Tiny Blanco, a known bookie, was waiting outside, and Mickey paid him. Then he ambled down the street and went into a real estate office, then a woman agent took him to look at three houses. He bought the best one, a duplex and two rental apartments and a garage."

"How much?"

"Just a guess: a million and a half. And the only other way he could have come into that much money, I figure, is to murder his mother, who's quite well off. But she's still alive. The other good news is, he's not going to need your client's money, not until he makes a few more bad bets, anyway, which he will surely do."

Mickey met Geraldine Conner in the bar at the River Café, the swankiest place in Brooklyn. She had dressed for the occasion and looked great. They had a champagne cocktail, then they were shown to their table, overlooking the East River and Lower Manhattan.

"This is gorgeous!" she said. "I've heard about this place, but I've never been here."

They had a look at the menu. "You were the talk of the bank yesterday," she said. "I mean, nobody just walks in and deposits two million dollars in his personal checking account."

"Bankers talk, do they?"

"Just among themselves, not to anybody else."

"I bought a house yesterday," he said.

"A whole house?"

"A duplex and two rental apartments, not far from here."

"Oh, wow. You're having a good week!"

"I certainly am."

"When do you close?"

"Tomorrow."

"That's fast."

"My lawyer is handling it." He looked at his watch. "He'd better be reading the contract right now."

They dined and drank until ten o'clock. "I'd ask you back to my place for a nightcap," Mickey said, "but there's no furniture yet."

"Well, we'd better go back to my house," Gerry said. "My roommates have got a rental in the Hamptons, and they're out there."

"Invitation accepted," Mickey said.

Mickey stumbled out of her place around two AM and walked back to his mother's house, all aglow.

Jack Coulter sat at a table in the sun and worked on his tan. His nose, under the plastic protector, had become very white. A waiter brought him a second cup of coffee, and a busboy took away his breakfast dishes. His phone rang. He looked around, found nobody within range, and answered it.

"Yeah?"

"Johnny. You know who this is."

"Yeah. You're late, Vinnie."

"My boss says to tell you there won't be any more money."

"Did he say why?"

"He doesn't have to. He's the boss. Me, I figure he thinks you've gotten all your money back and more, and he ain't giving you no more."

"You tell him for me that I want last week's vig and a refund of the mil I gave you in the beginning in my bank account by noon tomorrow."

"Or what?"

"Or you're both dead within a week, that's what. And if you think I'm kidding, you're already dead."

"Johnny . . ."

"You see, I know exactly where you both are, but you don't know where I am. Got it?"

"Yeah, but . . ."

"You've got the message," Jack said. "Deliver it, and if he doesn't come through by noon tomorrow, get a head start on your funeral arrangements. Both of you. Goodbye, and I **mean** goodbye." Jack hung up. He didn't run, and he wasn't afraid. He knew what he had to do and how to do it, and they couldn't get at him.

Vinnie, the bookie, didn't walk—he walked **fast** from his position at the post, out of the track, and across the parking lot to an Airstream trailer parked at the outer edge, next to an old-fashioned telephone pole that was festooned with aerials and satellite dishes. He knocked on the door.

"Who is it?" a muffled voice replied.

"It's Vinnie. I gotta talk to him."

There was some muttering, then the sound of something being unlocked, and the door opened. "Get in here," a man said from behind the door.

Vinnie got in there, and the door slammed and was locked behind him. His boss, Manny, sat at the breakfast table of the trailer, which sported three phones and a calculator. A man was seated across the table, packing stacks of hundreds into air-shipping boxes.

"What?" Manny inquired, not looking up.

"You might want to hear this alone," Vinnie said.

Now Manny looked at him. "Are you serious?"

"Oh, yeah."

Manny tapped the money packer on the arm and jerked a thumb toward the opposite end of the table. "Lose yourself, but don't go out."

The man did the best he could, given the confines of the trailer.

"Sit," Manny said. He had always been a man of few words.

Vinnie sat. "Johnny Fratelli called."

"I figured, when he didn't get his money."

"Manny, I'm going to tell you exactly what he said, to the best of my recall. I want you to remember that I didn't say any of this. Johnny did."

"Right."

Vinnie repeated his conversation with John Fratelli, word for word, with the emphasis in all the right places.

"He's kidding right? He thinks he can threaten **us**?"

"Manny, when we was in the joint together, Johnny had a reputation. Well, he had more than one reputation, but the big one was about threats."

"What about threats?"

"He didn't make threats. He made promises, and he always kept them. **Always."**

Manny looked just a little impressed. "Yeah?"

"I saw it happen time and again, over fifteen years. He never failed to come through, not once. If Johnny said it was going to happen, it happened."

Manny made a swallowing noise and looked around, as if for help. He was unaccustomed to being threatened. He had known Johnny Fratelli well enough to believe what Vinnie was saying.

"You know where he is?"

"No," Vinnie said. "He always uses throwaways, then he throws them away. The important thing is: he knows where you and I are. He knows where this trailer is. Can you imagine how much money you would lose if this trailer got burned up?"

"Did he say he would do that?"

"No, he just said we have until noon tomorrow for his mil and the vig from last week to turn up in his account."

"Or what?"

"He didn't say how, just that it would happen. Then he said, 'Get a head start on your funeral arrangements. Both of you.'"

"Pay him," Manny said. "And make sure the amount is correct." He pointed at the money packer and jerked a thumb toward the unpacked money. "Beat it, Vinnie."

Vinnie beat it. And he was already on the phone to the money guy, with instructions.

12

Mickey woke early, then went to the kitchen upstairs and made his mother's favorite, scrambled eggs, for breakfast. He set everything on the tray, then warmed the coffeepot with hot water before pouring in the coffee and replacing the lid. He found a little vase and put into it a single rose, from a bunch on the windowsill, then he poured a glass of freshly squeezed orange juice, set the **New York Times** on the tray, and carried it into her bedroom, where she was just waking up.

"What's this?" she asked as he set the tray beside her, then pressed the button that raised her bed to a sitting position.

"Just breakfast," he said, setting the tray on her lap. "It's the least I can do."

"Use the money well," she said, "but not on

the horses. That's over, or your inheritance ends there."

"Gotcha. May I have some advice?"

"Well, that's new. What do you need?"

"Are you happy with your stockbroker?"

"Very."

"May I have his name and number? I want to invest about half the money."

"His card is in my center desk drawer," she said. "Take his advice."

"I'll do that."

"What are you doing with the rest of the money?"

"Well, I bought a house." He gave her the address. "A duplex and two rental apartments and a garage."

"Good move. I suppose you'll need a car to fill the garage."

"It crossed my mind."

"There's also a card in my desk for a man named Herman Goldsmith. He deals in high-end cars, independently; he'll find you what you want."

"Great. I need some clothes, too. The rest I'll spend on wine, women, and song."

"You're entitled. Now, let me eat my breakfast and read my newspaper before the eggs get cold."

Mickey called the broker and made an appointment, then he got ready to go out. He was early, so he called Herman Goldsmith. "I'm Michael O'Brien. My mother, Louise, sent me to you."

"Great. Nice lady. What can I do for you?" the man asked.

"I want a Mercedes S-Class four-door, loaded."

"What color?"

"A nice shade of silver would be good."

"Interior leather?"

"Tan or dark brown."

"Give me your cell number, and I'll get back to you."

They both hung up, and Mickey went to see the broker. An hour later he was a growth-oriented shareholder.

He was waiting for the elevator when Herman Goldsmith called.

"Check your e-mail. You'll find pictures and equipment lists for three Mercedes S 560s. One of them has the sports engine and package, which is very expensive. They are available immediately. Call me." He hung up.

Mickey let the elevator slide and made himself comfortable in the broker's waiting room while he checked out the photos of the cars and their prices. He called Herman back. "I'd like the one with the dark brown leather."

"Where do you want it delivered?"

Mickey gave him the address of his new house. "What time?"

"An hour and a half. The guy will give you a package with the invoice, title, and other stuff. You give him a check for the amount of the invoice. My company name is on it."

"Thank you, Herman."

"Anytime. My best to Louise." They both hung up.

As Mickey left the building he saw something he had seen when he had left the house: a gray van with the name of a plumber emblazoned on its panels. It had darkened windows, too. Odd, he thought, that he should see the same van in two different places on the same morning.

He walked down the street for a block and stopped before a store window that gave him the reflection of the street behind him. The van pulled out of its parking spot, drove past him for a couple of blocks, then made a turn and was gone. He had gotten spooked for nothing. Besides, who would give a damn how he was spending his morning?

Mickey was at his new house with the garage door open, when his new car showed up on time. He did a walk-around with the deliverer, pronounced it okay, and wrote a check. The guy gave him the envelope with the window-sticker, the title, and the invoice marked **Paid**.

He showed Mickey how to set up the electronics, then left. Mickey got into the car and started it. The thing made a beautiful noise.

Jack Coulter turned on his iPhone at 11:00 AM and logged onto his offshore bank account. No sign of the money he had demanded. Well, they had another hour. He sat by the pool until noon, then called back; the money was there, all of it. It paid to be remembered as someone who kept his promises, he reflected.

Hillary came down from their apartment at the Breakers, and they ordered a good lunch.

"I've had some interesting news this morning," she said over her lobster salad.

"Tell me."

"We've had an offer for the company," she said.

"That **is** interesting."

"My share would be just over a billion dollars, and that's after taxes."

Jack had just stuffed a large piece of lobster into his mouth and he chewed it carefully for a while before swallowing. He considered that the delay might make him appear thoughtful. "That's very nice," he said finally, keeping calm. "Is it a first offer?"

"Yes."

"Turn it down," he replied.

"Are you sure?"

"Always turn down a first offer. Ask for twenty percent more, then take fifteen."

"All right," she said, picking up her phone.

Jack went to the men's room to give her some privacy. When he came back, she was smiling. "They went for it," she said. "You made me a million and a half dollars more on the transaction. That's your commission: a million and a half."

"Sweetheart, you don't need to do that."

"Yes, I do," she said, "so don't argue with me!" She kissed him.

"You win," he said.

13

Mickey was back in the real estate office in time for the closing. Marge had taken care of everything; all he had to do was sign a lot of stuff, then call the bank and do the wire transfer.

"Congratulations," Marge said when they were done. "You're officially a homeowner. When do you move in?"

"Hey, wait a minute. I don't have a stick of furniture."

"I've got a friend in SoHo who sells and rents all sorts of furniture."

"Rents?"

"For theatrical productions and movies. She'll sell you anything she's got, right off the floor, and the prices are good."

"How about you be my decorator?" he said.

"I do that sort of thing," she said. "How much do you want to spend?"

“How much stuff will twenty grand get me?”

“**Fully** furnished?”

“Yep.”

“Better start with fifty thousand. That will get you the basics, and you can fill in the gaps later.”

“You do it,” he said.

“You’d trust me to do that?”

“You’ll do a better job than I would.” He unsnapped a key from the ring she had given him. “Let me know when it’s done.”

“It’ll be faster than you think. Tell you what, give me three days, then you can come and take a look at what I’ve done.”

“You’ve got a deal,” he said.

“I get ten percent of what you spend.”

“Done. Call me, if you need more.” He gave her a credit card. “Put it on this. It has a zero balance.”

“You want art, too?”

“Sure. You pick it out.”

“I’ll need to spend another fifteen grand on that.”

“Okay. One thing I want is an electric bed. Two electric singles with king sheets and a duvet on top.”

“I can do that. You come to the house at five o’clock on Friday. No peeking before that.”

“You’ve got a date,” he said. “Then I’ll buy you dinner.”

“Done.”

* * *

When Stone came down to work, Bob Cantor was waiting for him. "Let me save you some money and pull my guys off Mickey O'Brien," he said.

"Why?"

"He's bought a house, and a woman is decorating it for him. He opened an account with a stockbroker. He bought a new Mercedes S560. He's not after your client's money, at the moment. Why pay for the moment?"

"Well, my client is out of town anyway," Stone said. "Pull 'em off and give Joan the bill."

"I'll have somebody check on him once a week. If there's a change in his intentions, we'll get right on it."

"All right, all right."

Bob left Stone and the other Bob, the Labrador retriever, keeping each other company, the Lab in his usual spot by the fireplace.

Jack Coulter was wakened by the sound of the house phone in their apartment at the Breakers. Hillary answered. "Yes?" she said. "Yes?" she went on. "Yes!" she cried. "Please hold." She put her hand over the phone. "Jack, they've come up to a billion three for our share."

Jack's eyes opened. "Yes," he said.

"We'll take it," she said. "When do we close? All right." She hung up. "The buyer is in a hurry. We close in a week."

"If I'd know he was in a hurry I'd have asked for more," Jack said.

"You're so smart!"

"I don't know anything I didn't learn up the river," Jack said. "In the joint, negotiating is a daily practice. You get good at it."

"Maybe I should have gone to Sing Sing, instead of Bryn Mawr," she said, laughing.

"I like you the way Bryn Mawr made you," Jack replied, sitting up. "Can we have some celebratory eggs?"

"What are we going to do with it, Jack?"

"With what?"

"All that money."

"You have a brokerage account; put it in there."

"I'm not crazy about those people. I'd like somebody a little more . . ."

"Aggressive? I'll think of something. Give me a little time."

Stone was having his mid-morning coffee when Joan buzzed him. "Jack Coulter on one for you."

Stone stabbed the button. "Morning, Jack, are you all right?"

"Me? Of course. Oh, you mean Mickey O'Brien."

"Yes. He's not a threat at the moment. He's come into some money, and he's too busy spending it to think about you."

"Coming into some money is why I'm calling."

"Did you hit big with your bookie?"

"No, I took my money back from those people."

Stone's jaw dropped. "They let you cash out? I would never have believed it. Those guys never let go of money. How'd you manage it?"

"I asked them nicely."

Stone burst out laughing. "What does that mean?"

"It means I threatened them if I didn't have the money back the next day. In prison, I learned to keep my promises, so they believed me. The reason I called was to ask your advice about investing a windfall."

"Are we talking about your million from the bookie?"

"No, it's a bit more than that. Hillary is selling the family business, and after a little negotiation, we settled for a billion three."

"For the whole company? That sounds low."

"No, her sisters are involved, too. That's just her share, after taxes."

Stone was flabbergasted. "Forgive me, Jack, but I don't often hear that kind of number bandied about, especially after taxes."

"Me, either. Now, Hillary and I don't think

her broker has been doing a terrific job for her, and I was wondering if you have a recommendation. We'd like someone fairly aggressive."

"Well, yes, I know somebody." Stone told him about Triangle Investments, his company with Mike Freeman and Charley Fox. "Charley is an ex–Goldman Sachs guy, whose specialty is mergers and acquisitions. He keeps an eye out for growth companies. We try to get in early. That's where my money is. Are you in town?"

"No, but we'll be back in tomorrow. Can we have lunch with you and your colleague, the day after?"

"Certainly."

"We're closing in about a week, so we'll want to move fast, so as not to lose income."

"I'll tell Charley that," Stone said.

"Okay. I'll see you, say, the day after tomorrow?"

"The Grill at what used to be the Four Seasons, at twelve-thirty."

"See you there. I'll introduce you to my new nose." Jack hung up.

Stone made a conference call to Charley Fox and Mike Freeman.

"Morning, gentlemen," Stone said. "Are you both in New York?"

"I am," Charley said.

"I'm in the Gulfstream," Mike replied, "over the Atlantic, on the way home."

"Are you both free for lunch the day after tomorrow, at the Grill?"

They both responded in the affirmative.

"I want you to meet some interesting clients of mine, who would like to invest some money with us."

"I don't know, Stone," Charley said. "It's time-consuming, dealing with more people than just the three of us."

"How much does he want to invest?" Mike asked.

"One billion, three hundred million dollars."

"Ignore Charley, Stone. We'll both see you at lunch."

14

Mickey O'Brien called a company he used to work for, driving limos part-time, back when he was a patrolman. They had a division called Chauffeurs Unlimited, who furnished drivers for your own car. He arranged to meet one at his house, then got into the rear seat of his new Mercedes. "Ralph Lauren, Madison and Seventy-Second," he said to the driver

"Yes, sir, Mr. O'Brien."

In due course they pulled up to the old Rhinelander Mansion, which now housed the home store of Mr. Lauren. Mickey went upstairs to men's suits and picked out a half dozen and a tuxedo. He had always been a perfect size 40 regular, so only the trouser lengths had to be fixed. He picked out another half dozen tweed jackets and a blue blazer, as many odd trousers, then he went downstairs to look at shoes while they did the trouser cuffs. He picked out a half dozen pairs of shoes, two of them very expensive alligator, then he bought some socks and sweaters.

When everything was ready he directed them to be put into the trunk of the Mercedes, then headed down to East Fifty-Seventh Street to Turnbull & Asser, where he ordered two dozen shirts to be made, plus a selection of neckties and some ready-made things, since the custom shirts took a couple of months.

Back in the car, he made a reservation for two at Daniel, then headed downtown and called Marge, who was working on his new house. "Hey."

"Hey."

"Are you at the house?"

"I am, and working like a beaver."

"I've got a trunkful of clothes I'd like to drop off. Can you put them in my closet for me?"

"Dressing room," she said. "You don't have a closet, you have a dressing room. I guess you missed that on the tour."

"All the better."

"I don't want you in the house yet, though."

"I'll send the driver up with the things, then I'll pick you up at seven-thirty. Where will you be?"

"Here. I brought a change of clothes to save time, and I'll use your shower."

"Do I have towels, yet?"

"You do. You have just about everything. I'm

just arranging with a couple of guys to move things."

"Okay, see you at seven-thirty."

"Where are we dining?"

"It's a surprise."

"Whatever you say.

He was driven downtown. Then, while the driver carried everything into the house, he sat in the front seat and played with the electronics, setting up his satellite radio and selecting stations.

Stone, Charley Fox, and Mike Freeman rose to greet Jack and Hillary Coulter. Stone was struck by the difference in Jack's face. His nose was just as long, but narrower, lending refinement to his face. His previous schnoz had suffered from his prison experience. There was still a little redness, but not enough to matter. His graying hair had grown and was handsomely barbered. Stone introduced everybody, and they all sat down and chatted while they looked at menus and ordered.

"Is the figure you mentioned to Stone still correct?" Charley asked, to get the ball rolling.

"Yes," Jack replied.

"I suggest you put three hundred into a money market fund, then we invest the remainder."

"All right," Jack said, and Hillary nodded.

"With the rest I want to put you into one startup and another outfit that will go public this year, then we'll start hunting for new buys. We'll do so in such a way that we'll be investing alongside you. I wouldn't put you into anything we didn't think enough of to invest in it ourselves."

Charley talked for a half hour uninterrupted, then lunch arrived and they resumed chatting.

"We'd like debit cards to use against the money market fund," Jack said.

"Of course. May I ask, what are you doing with your other assets?"

"We'll leave them where they are for a while, I think. At some time in the future, we may want to move them to the new account."

"That's fine," Charley said. After lunch, everybody went home feeling satisfied with how it had gone.

Mickey and Marge sat in the center of the floor at Daniel, and dined grandly.

"I've never been here," Marge said, "living in Brooklyn. I like it."

"We'll come here often then."

"I should tell you that I'm divorced," she said.

"Who isn't?"

"Just once, though."

"Twice for me. It wasn't their fault. Living with a cop isn't easy."

"Kids?"

"Nope. You?"

"No. I'm thirty-six," she said.

"I'm fifty. That's how old you have to be to retire on a full pension from the NYPD."

"Anything else you want to know?" she asked.

"You mean, like, your bra size?"

She laughed. "You can figure that out for yourself."

"I'll look forward to that."

They finished their dinner and were on dessert.

"Why don't we have a cognac at your place?" Marge asked.

"I'm not due to move in until tomorrow."

"I have a surprise for you. It's ready now, everything in its place."

"In that case," Mickey said, waving for a check, "let's have a cognac at my place."

"Love to."

Mickey woke early, as he usually did. Marge was sprawled beside him, her blond hair splayed over her pillow. He eased his way out of bed and into the silk robe she had bought for him, then he stood and looked around the room. It was perfect. He loved the dressing room with his new suits and jackets hanging there. He would give his old stuff to Goodwill.

He walked around the apartment and looked at what he had first seen the night before, but with an owner's eyes. It was remarkable how everything suited him. It was as if he'd done his own shopping, but with better taste.

He figured out how to use the coffee maker, made them some, and took it upstairs.

She was sitting up in bed, the covers only up to her waist. He set her coffee on the bedside table, shucked off his robe, and climbed in beside her. They clinked coffee cups.

"It's absolutely perfect," he said. "I feel lucky to live here."

"That's how I wanted you to feel," she said.

The phone at his bedside buzzed.

"That's the front door," she said. "Just pick it up and talk."

He did so. "Hello?"

"Hey, pal, it's Tiny. How you doin'?"

"I'm not here," Mickey replied. "Try to remember that."

"But I got a horse for you."

"Eat it yourself," Mickey said, then hung up.

Marge laughed. "I won't ask who that was."

"A guy I'd like to forget is alive," Mickey said.

Tiny squeezed his bulk back into his car. "Can you believe that guy?" He asked nobody in particular.

"Who?"

"Mickey O'Brien. I carried him for years, and

now that he's flush he don't want to bet with me no more."

"You made a lot of money on Mick, Tiny," the man reminded him.

"All the reason to make a lot more," Tiny reasoned. "And I intend to."

"If he won't bet, how you going to do that?" the driver asked.

"I'll figure it out," Tiny replied. "He's always been mine, and he's going to keep being mine."

15

Vinnie sat in his box seat at the post at Hialeah and, using his binoculars, watched the herd turn into the home stretch. He glanced at the board to get the final odds and was pleased. His bets were well-placed. His phone rang, but he waited for the winner to cross the finish line before he answered.

"It's Vinnie, talk to me." He had a pencil and pad ready to take the bet.

"It's Manny," he said.

Vinnie winced. Manny didn't call often, and when he did, it was always about something Vinnie didn't want to do. "Morning, Manny."

"That guy," Manny said.

Vinnie knew who he was talking about but pretended not to. "Which guy?"

"That guy I just made a gift of a mil."

"Manny, it wasn't a gift. It was his money, and we made a bundle off it while we had it."

"I want it back."

"You want **his** money back?"

"You hard of hearing?"

"No, and I'm afraid I heard what you just said."

"Tell me what I just said."

"You said you want a client's money back."

"See? You can hear just fine."

"Yeah, but I don't believe what I'm hearing."

"You want to come over here and have me explain it to you in person?"

"Manny, can I tell you some things?"

"If you can do it in less than a minute of my time."

"This guy took care of Eduardo Buono in Sing Sing for over twenty years, and Eduardo never took a punch for all of that time. He lived like a king, and Johnny was his prince."

"So what? I still want his money."

"I told you how Johnny and I communicated."

"With throwaways, so what?"

"I met with him just once, in a diner, where he handed over his mil. So, I never knew where he was, and I don't know now."

"Find him," Manny said.

"Manny, this guy is very, very smart. Who could go into Sing Sing broke and come out with millions?"

"Eduardo's millions. And Fratelli ain't the kind of guy to spend it all. He's still got it, and more. I want everything he's got."

"Manny, you call me up and tell me you want back a guy's money who dealt with us straight, and then decided he wanted out, for whatever reason. And now, you want . . ."

"I know his reason," Manny said, "and I know how to find him."

"You mean, you know how **I** can find him."

"Your hearing is still good, Vinnie."

"And how do I do that?"

"You know Tiny Blanco, in Brooklyn?"

"Yeah, or I used to anyway. He's a real piece of shit."

"I don't care what he is. He's got a client named Mickey O'Brien . . ."

"A cop. I knew him, too; degenerate gambler."

"Ex-cop. He wants Eduardo's money, too, and he knows how to find Johnny Fratelli."

"So, you want me to call Tiny Blanco and tell him we want his client? Then he's going to want a big cut."

"You're right, and that's why you don't call him. You call somebody else who knows Mickey from when he was a cop and find out where he lives. Then you have a conversation with Mickey."

"What's Mickey's motivation for telling me where to find Fratelli?"

"'Motivation'? His motivation is he gets to keep

living and walking around on two legs without crutches."

"Okay, I'll make inquiries."

"Get your ass on a plane to New York, and call me when you've got your hand on Mickey O'Brien's throat. Your number two can handle Hialeah, until you're back."

"I won't be responsible for what he does while I'm gone."

"I'll see to that. Call me when you get to New York." Manny hung up.

Vinnie sighed. His number two walked up and tapped him on the shoulder.

"Yeah?"

"I got a call from Manny's guy. He says you're expected in New York."

"If you screw up while I'm gone, Manny's going to cut your balls off. You know that."

The backup guy knew that.

16

Marge Twist amazed Mickey O'Brien. Day after day, she came to the house and cooked for him. She found him a daily maid; she rented the two empty apartments. And she was always ready for sex, any kind he liked—and he liked everything. So did she: front, back, upside down, it didn't matter, she loved it. It occurred to Mickey that, since he had never had a woman like this, it might be something to do with the fact he was rich. Every day she brought a few things with her, and soon, she was using half his dressing room.

He was also humping Gerry, the bank teller, a couple of times a week. He was on Viagra, like, all the time. Being rich was fun.

Then one day, when Marge was at work, there was a knock on his door, and a guy in a black raincoat stepped inside and put a gun to Mickey's forehead. "Where's Johnny Fratelli?" he asked.

"How the hell should I know?"

The guy in the black raincoat cocked the weapon. "One last chance to cure your memory failure."

"I'll tell you everything I know," Mickey said. "I was walking down Lexington Avenue a few weeks ago, and I passed Johnny on the street. I recognized him and followed him. When I got a chance, I turned him around and hit him in the face with a blackjack. Some passersby screamed for the cops and an ambulance, and I beat it out of there. I heard later than he had checked into a private hospital somewhere on the East Side, but I could never find him, because I didn't have a name. I still don't, and that's the God's honest truth." Mikey hoped the lie didn't show on his face.

"If I don't believe you, I'm supposed to kill you," the guy said.

"Well, I hope to God you believe me, because that's all I know."

"Oh, another question: How'd you get so rich all of a sudden?"

"My mother gave me my inheritance early. It's about gone now."

The guy nodded and turned to go. "I'll pass it on."

Mickey closed the door behind him and locked it, breathing hard. "What the hell was that?" he asked himself aloud.

* * *

Manny picked up the phone. "Yeah?"

"It's Vinnie. We braced Mickey O'Brien. He told us he passed Fratelli on the street, on Lexington Avenue, and slugged him with a blackjack and then had to run for it. He heard Fratelli was in a private hospital, but he couldn't find him, because he didn't have a name. We believe the guy was telling the truth."

"How'd he get so rich?"

"His mother gave him his inheritance early, and he blew most of it. The consensus is, he's got nothing left."

"I want his money, and Fratelli's."

"Manny, I just explained he's blown his inheritance. He's got nothing. And he doesn't know what name Fratelli is using, so he can't find him."

"I don't care, I want the money."

"Whose money?"

"Everybody's."

"Well, you can't have it, Manny, because it ain't there to have, and nobody knows who's got it or where he is or what his name is."

"I want the money."

"No." Vinnie didn't think anybody had ever said that word to Manny—not anybody who had survived the experience—because he could feel the earth shake all the way to Brooklyn.

"Now, Manny, do you still want me working for you at the track?"

"Yeah, sure. And I want the money."

"I can't give you the money, nobody can. Now, unless you accept that right now, I won't be coming back to Hialeah, not to Florida, either. I'll get out and take what I've got with me, and you can find some other guy to look into it and tell you the same goddamned thing. What's it going to be?"

Manny thought about it. "All right, come back to Hialeah."

"Are you going to leave me alone about this money?"

"Maybe."

"Not good enough, Manny. I want you off my back; you're too heavy."

"Oh, fuck it. Come on home and get your ass back to work. Your backup guy fucks up every day."

"I'm going to rest for a day. I'll fly home tomorrow and I'll be back at the post the day after."

"Okay."

"Goodbye." Vinnie hung up the phone. He was in the last phone booth on Fifth Avenue, he reckoned. As he stepped out of it he saw Johnny Fratelli. He froze. What was he going to do? He couldn't brace Johnny; he'd get his head handed to him. So he followed, and at a respectful distance.

Fratelli was skinnier, he thought, and he was wearing expensive clothes. Then, at an intersection, Fratelli made to cross the street and looked both ways. The image of Johnny dissolved before Vinnie's eyes. From the back, it was Fratelli; from the front and side, it was somebody else.

Vinnie went back to his hotel on Sixth Avenue, flung himself onto the bed, and drifted off. Before unconsciousness came, he resolved not to tell Manny about the encounter; Manny would just put him on another plane to New York, and he'd had more than enough of New York.

Mickey O'Brien went down to Little Italy and found the alley where Tiny Blanco kept an office. As it happened, Tiny stepped into the alley as Mickey approached. Mickey pulled his .38 Smith & Wesson from his ankle holster, walked up to Tiny, and stuck it under his chin. "What the fuck do you mean sending a guy with a gun to my house?"

"Hey, take it easy, Mick. He didn't shoot you, did he? You look okay to me."

"I don't like guns in my face. I don't like the way you operate. I don't like you. If you ever pull something else like that I'll put two in your brain, you hear me?"

"I hear you, Mick."

"And I know how to do it and get away with it."

"Okay, Mick. I read you loud and clear. It was Manny, the bookie from Florida, who wanted information."

"And you sent him to me?" Mick cocked the pistol.

"Never again!" Tiny said.

"You remember you said that," Mick replied. Then he walked away, having bled off the head of steam he had accumulated.

17

Jack Coulter called Stone Barrington, and Joan put him right through.

"Good morning, Jack. How are you?"

"Very well, thank you, Stone. I want to thank you for putting me in touch with Charley Fox. I was very impressed with him."

"I'm glad to hear it, Jack. Charley has certainly done very well for me."

"I wired the funds to him an hour ago and got a confirmation right back, saying he'll send me a list of what he buys for me and instructions as to how to check my account online."

"That's the way we do it. You don't have to read the papers or watch CNBC to know where you are."

"Tell me, what do you hear about Mickey O'Brien?"

"Funny. My guy, Bob Cantor, who's been doing

surveillance on Mickey, was in here this morning. I'd had his people watching him around the clock—you'll get a bill for that—but he recommended easing off to one day a week, which was yesterday, and that's when something happened."

"What happened?"

"Mickey was called on at his new house by a guy dressed in a black raincoat and a black hat, and Bob's guy on site recognized him as a known hitman named Willie Pasco. Do you know him?"

"Never heard of him," Jack said. "But unless he's my age, or older, I wouldn't."

"Anyway, Pasco was only in the house for a minute or two, then he left. We wondered if Mickey had been hit, but a couple of minutes later, he left the house looking angry and took a cab to Little Italy, where he braced the guy who used to be his bookie, one Tiny Blanco, stuck a gun in his face in an alley and talked to him earnestly for about a minute, then he got out of there, leaving Tiny in a near-fainting state."

"What do you make of all that?"

"Bob thinks somebody hired Pasco to hit Mickey, or at least frighten him, and that made Mickey mad. I guess he thought Tiny ordered the bracing and went off his head."

"And how does that relate to me?"

"We don't know. I'd hoped the names might ring a bell or two for you, and you could tell us."

"No, they don't."

"Oh, there was one other piece of the puzzle: one of Bob's people recognized a guy from Florida named Vinnie, who was in town and in touch with Tiny the day before. Does that mean anything?"

"Yes, it does. A bookie named Vinnie, who works out of Hialeah, was the guy I placed a bundle of money with and got five percent a week."

"I remember you mentioning that."

"But when they failed to pay the interest one week, I demanded that money and my bundle back and gave them twenty-four hours to comply. I had a reputation in prison for keeping my promises, and I guess they figure it was less trouble to give the money back than to worry about me."

"Who is the other party in 'they'?"

"Oh, Vinnie works for a guy named Manny who runs the mob's South Florida interests. My money would have been funneled through Vinnie and him to somebody else."

"Do you think Vinnie would have put out a hit on you?"

"No, but Manny would, if he was pissed off. He'd have had Vinnie hire somebody. Now all this is making sense."

"I'm sorry, I'm missing something. What would Vinnie—or, rather, Manny—want from you?"

"Manny would probably want my money back. He's the greedy sort. And in order to get it back he'd have to find me, and that means he needs to know my new name. Vinnie knows me only as Fratelli. Mickey O'Brien is the only person I can think of who knows that name."

"Ah," Stone said. "I sort of understand. Is there anything you want Bob's people to do about this? I don't mean anything drastic."

"No. I need to think about the whole thing and a way to throw a monkey wrench into their works."

"Well, you've got your new nose working for you."

Jack laughed. "Yes, there is that."

"Let me know if you need anything else."

"Thanks, Stone, I think I know how to handle it. Do you have an address for Mickey?"

Stone gave it to him. "Oh, and Mickey has a girlfriend living with him named Marge: she was his real estate agent on the house."

"Got it. Thank you again, Stone." Jack hung up. He had to sleep on this before he did anything, but it was already clear that he had to do **something**.

Stone called Bob Cantor. "Hey. My client was on the phone this morning, the one who's worried about Mick O'Brien."

"What's with that, anyway?" Cantor asked.

Stone took a deep breath. "I can't tell you much. Let's just say they knew each other in another life, and Mickey is the only one who knows about that life."

"Okay, I buy that. Do you think he wants something done to Mickey? I mean, you and I don't deal in that, right?"

"Very right."

"Is your client capable of dealing with it directly?"

"My client is capable of wringing Mickey's neck like a chicken's. But we don't want blood in the streets of Brooklyn, especially on my client's hands. He's an upstanding citizen."

"Does this thing between them have anything to do with that big robbery at an apartment on Fifth Avenue? I mean, when I was redoing the security system, I saw Mickey there. He was one of the investigators."

"My client attended that party." Never mind that Jack was the **host** of that party, Stone said to himself. "Mickey might have seen him there on the night."

"And he would have seen Mickey."

"Possibly."

"I'm getting the feeling that I'm tiptoeing a little too close to the edge here."

Stone remained silent.

"Okay, let's scrap that theory."

"It could work, as long as it's only a theory and not spread around."

"I see," Bob said. At least, he thought he saw.

18

Bob Cantor thought about this thing for a while. He'd gone as far as he could with Stone, maybe further than he should have. Maybe he'd see what he could find out without consulting him. After all, what people want in this sort of case is a result; even if they didn't want to deal with the means.

Bob knew Tiny Blanco from his days as a cop, when Tiny was muscle for his predecessor. Tiny wasn't stupid, but he was a bully—that is, he enjoyed siccing his boys on some hapless son of a bitch who couldn't cover his bets. Bob viewed bullying as a weakness, a way inside a man's head.

Bob drove his van down to Little Italy and put it in a parking garage around the corner from the alley where Tiny's business operated. He remembered something about Tiny: he always lunched alone at the same Italian restaurant, probably because he didn't want anybody to see how much he ate. He sat near the kitchen at a table behind a screen, sheltered further between his table and the kitchen by a tall piece of furniture that held the silverware in pigeonholes.

Bob walked down the street to the next alley where the restaurant, Luigi's, was situated. He walked past the place slowly, casing it. The screen was still there. Bob checked his watch: a quarter past one; Tiny was probably there now. The place was more than half empty, catering as it did to an earlier lunch crowd. Bob walked back and into the restaurant, grabbing a menu on his way. He sat down at the table next to the screen and listened. Judging from the noises being made, either Tiny was behind it, or they were keeping pigs in the place now.

He leaned close to the screen. "Hello, Tiny," he said.

The noises stopped for a moment, while Tiny tried to place the voice, then he chewed some more and swallowed. "Whozzat?" he asked.

"An old acquaintance," Bob replied.

"Whaddaya want?"

"Just the answers to a couple of questions."

"Not now, I'm eating."

"Yeah, I know. I could hear the noises out in the street."

"Maybe you would like to ask your questions to some friends of mine."

"No, Tiny, just you. Give me straight answers, and I'll be gone. Give me crooked answers, and I'll shut you down, take your money, and pull out your phones. How'd you like to do a couple of years on Rikers? I hear they have a very fine chef there."

"What do you want?" Tiny said, enunciating more clearly without a slab of veal in the way.

"You sent Willie Pasco to see Mickey O'Brien. Who told you to send him and why?"

"You don't want to mess with that," Tiny said. "Those people play for keeps."

"Then what's a small-time bookie like you messing with them?"

"I got a request," Tiny said.

"That brings us back to my original question," Bob said. "Who from and what for? And if I don't get an answer I like, you're going to hear the sound of police sirens before the next minute has passed."

"From a guy in Florida," Tiny said. "Manny runs things for the boys down there."

"Keep going."

"Manny Fiore. Every buck off a track or a card game in South Florida passes through Manny Fiore's hands."

"Where does he work out of?"

"He has an old trailer parked at the back of the parking lot of the Hialeah, one of them Streamers, or something."

"Airstreamer?"

"Yeah, that's it. Now get off my back, or I'll call for some help."

"And you'd need it," Bob said. He slid out of his seat, left a twenty for the waiter, and left the restaurant.

Tiny was left wondering if he still had company. Finally, he pulled back the screen an inch and looked. Nobody there.

Back in his van, Bob Cantor called Stone.

"Yes, Bob?"

"I got a name for somebody who might be involved with trying to find your client."

"And that would be . . . ?"

"Manny Fiore, who deals with all the betting money in South Florida." He told Stone about the Airstream trailer.

"I don't guess you'd want to take a hop down to Florida and check him out."

"He's the kind of guy you don't want to check out," Bob said. "He hears somebody is looking into him, and first thing you know, the looker has a gun in his ear, and somebody's pulling the trigger."

"Then don't go to Florida," Stone said.

"Exactly what I had in mind."

"I'll mention the name to my client and see if it rings a bell."

"Okay, but don't ring any bells while you're doing it," Bob said. "People get hurt that way."

"Thanks, Bob."

Stone called Jack Coulter.

"Yes, Stone?"

"When you were in Florida, did you ever hear of somebody called Manny Fiore?"

"Certainly. Everybody who knows anything about the mob in South Florida knows that name. He's one of the people who handled my money. And it wouldn't have been refunded, if he hadn't approved."

"He's been looking into you, I hear."

"I'm sorry to hear it, but not surprised."

"He works out of an Airstream trailer in the parking lot at the Hialeah track."

"Ah."

"You think he wants another shot at your money?"

"I think he probably regrets giving it back. It's not really the sort of thing those guys do."

"How'd you manage it?"

"I threatened him, and he took it seriously."

"Jack, don't threaten mob guys. You could get hurt again that way."

"Thanks for the advice. I'll take care of it." Jack hung up.

* * *

Stone called Bob Cantor back. "The information you gave me meant something to my client. Is there anybody who can say you were asking about Fiore?"

"No, the guy I asked couldn't see me at the time."

"Whatever you say, Bob. I just don't want you to get caught up in this thing."

"I'm clear. Don't worry about it."

19

Jack Coulter dug out another throwaway phone from a desk drawer and called Vinnie.

"This is Vinnie."

"It's Johnny," Jack said.

"I don't much want to hear from you," Vinnie said.

"I just want to slip a flea into your ear. Are you where you usually are?"

"Nah, I'm in the big city, been here a couple days."

"You might want to extend your stay a little further," Jack said. "Be as far as possible from your friend in the trailer park."

"I'm far enough," Vinnie said. "Thanks."

"Be safe." Jack hung up. He gave some thought to old acquaintances from his former home up the Hudson. One came to mind. He called back

Vinnie. "One more thing, where might I find Solly White?"

"I'll give you a number."

"Shoot."

"It's a diner in Boca. He has lunch there most days. Don't mention I told you."

"I never mention anything to anybody," Jack said, then hung up. He checked his watch. Worth a try. He called the Boca number.

A woman answered, "Pizza Rumble."

"Lemme speak to Solly White," Jack said, reverting to his old voice.

The woman yelled, "Solly, for you!" She slammed the phone down hard.

It took Solly a moment to disengage from his pasta. "This is Solly," he said finally.

"This is a voice from the past," Jack said. "Don't mention any names."

"Gotcha, pal."

"Call me back at this number when you're done with lunch." He gave Solly another throwaway number.

"Half an hour," Solly said, then hung up.

The throwaway rang on schedule. "Yeah?"

"Well, I'll be fucked," Solly said. "I heard you had flown the coop, but I never . . ."

"You want some profitable work?"

"Depends on how profitable."

"Fifty G's. Half now, half when the work's done."

"That's an interesting number."

"Can you put your hands on some military-grade fireworks?"

"Depends. Who do I have to vaporize?"

"Nobody, just a trailer."

"Trailers are in trailer parks. Lots of people."

"This one is all by its lonesome. And it'll be empty of people at, say, three AM."

"Near here?"

"A few miles."

"When do you want the trailer to go away?"

"Tonight would be good. Tomorrow night at the latest."

"Where, exactly, is the thing parked?"

"At the south end of the parking lot at Hialeah track. You'll have to cut through a chain-link fence."

"Sounds doable. Let me swing by there and take a look. I'll call you back in a couple of hours."

"Good."

"How big a bang do you want to make?"

"Just big enough to shred the trailer. You can plant the plastic with a cell phone, then set if off from a distance."

"Good idea. I'll call you after I've checked it out."

"Right. This phone is okay for a couple more calls."

* * *

Jack watched an old movie on TV, then the phone rang. "Yeah?"

"It's doable. How about the money?"

"Give me an account number, and I'll wire you half now, the rest when it's done."

"Can you do it from offshore?"

"Yeah."

"Great, here's an offshore account number." He read out a series of numbers. "Offshore to Offshore, that's secure. I can get it done tonight. I've got the goods in stock.

"Don't call me in the middle of the night," Jack said.

"Switch your ringer off. I'll leave a message saying the flight took off on time. Then you wire the rest."

"As soon as the bank opens," Jack said. "Good luck."

"If I do my job right, I won't need luck."

Jack called a number in the Bahamas and gave some wiring instructions.

Solly spent a little more than an hour at his workbench. All he needed was some duct tape, a couple of brackets for backup, some wire, and a throwaway. Most of the time was spent setting up the phone to operate as planned.

Around one in the morning he drove through half-deserted surface streets to Hialeah and found his way to the wrong side of the parking lot fence. He immediately saw something he hadn't counted on. There was a light burning in the trailer. Somebody working late? Solly didn't like killing people, and he didn't take jobs where that was a serious possibility.

He shut down the engine, took a pair of track binoculars, 10x50s, and sighted through a trailer window. He could see half of a lamp burning, probably on a table or desk. He watched for a full five minutes and never saw a person or a moving shadow. He'd need a closer look.

Solly decided to cut through the fence there, behind a bush planted on the other side. He used his bolt cutters, and the work went quickly. He took his toolbox, already packed, from the trunk of the car, pressed down on the flap he had created, and stepped through the fence into the bush. Getting through the plant was harder than he had planned.

Then something happened. A second light went on inside the trailer. Solly crouched down into the plant, becoming one with it. Then came a sort of sucking noise, and the second light went out, then the first, then Solly heard the metallic sound of a door opening and closing, then silence.

Solly bulled his way through the fence, picked

up his toolbox and his bolt cutters, and ran for his car. He got in, started the engine, but did not turn on the headlights. He was pointed toward the trailer, but he didn't see anything. He opened the car door, stood outside, and looked around. The trailer had disappeared.

20

Jack Coulter was wakened from a deep sleep by a muffled ringing sound. He located it in his bottom bedside drawer and struggled out of bed while trying to find the right button. He staggered into his bathroom and closed the heavy door behind him and, finally, found the button. "What?"

"It's me," Solly said.

"I told you not to call me in the middle of the night. It's after three."

"I'm sorry, but something has gone wrong."

"What has gone wrong?"

"The trailer has disappeared."

"What are you talking about?"

"I mean, I installed the fixture and programmed the phone. Then I was getting back through the fence and heard a swooshing sound and saw the lights in the trailer go off. Then I got back to my car and when I turned around, the trailer was gone."

"It sounds like somebody was using the toilet in the trailer and then drove off," Jack said. "What do you have to do to get the thing to work?"

"I just call the number. When it answers, I press number one, then set a time, like two minutes, and it goes off two minutes later."

"Good. Do that."

"I can't do that!"

"Why not?"

"I don't know where the trailer is. There might be people nearby wherever it is."

"There is hardly going to be a crowd gathering anywhere at three in the morning. Do it!"

"I can't!"

"How about locating the phone electronically? Can you do that?"

"Well, I've got that 'Find My Phone' app. Maybe that would work."

"We'll never know until you try it."

"I'll call you back."

"No! Don't call me back. Text me."

"Oh, right." Solly hung up.

Jack sucked in deep breaths to get his heart rate down. "Jesus Christ," he said, to nobody in particular.

* * *

Solly opened the app and pressed the FIND button. The little wheel went round and round for a minute or so, then a map filled the screen with a red dot in the middle. He zoomed out far enough to see the racetrack on the map and figure the red dot was in another parking lot. Somebody who worked for Manny was just relocating it. He pressed the call button for the phone, then chose two minutes, then stared off into the distance toward the track. Two minutes later a fireball appeared off to the right of the track, and a second later, he felt a puff of wind and heard the explosion. Solly hoped like hell that the trailer had not been parked outside someplace where people lived.

He texted a message to Johnny's throwaway. **The flight took off a few minutes late, but it's gone.**

Jack had just gotten back to sleep when he was wakened by a dull chime. He opened the bottom drawer, retrieved and read Solly's confirmation message. Now he could relax. Except he couldn't get back to sleep.

Manny Fiore was lifted about six inches off his bed by a siren. It took him a moment to remember that the siren was the ringtone on his cell. He found his pants on the floor and groped for the phone. "Who the hell is this!" he screamed.

"It's me, boss. Sammy."

"Why the hell are you calling me at"—he checked the bedside clock—"three-thirty in the morning?"

"I thought you ought to know, boss. The trailer's gone."

"Gone? Somebody stole my trailer?"

"No, boss, I hooked up my truck to it and unhooked the wires, like you said, and I drove it over to lot five. I had just hooked it up and was driving away when the whole thing went up in smoke."

"The trailer caught fire?"

"No, boss, it exploded."

"**Exploded?** Why the fuck would it do that? What did you do to it?"

"All I did was unhook the cables, hook it up to my truck, drive it over to lot five, hook up the power and stuff, and drive away."

"Did you do anything else to it?"

"Oh, yeah, I used the toilet. You might want to get it serviced. Oh, never mind doing that now, it's gone."

"My whole trailer is gone."

"Now you got it, boss."

"No, I don't got it. Did the propane tank explode?"

"Well, that was kind of the second explosion,

after the first big one. It even made a mushroom cloud, and money was raining out of the cloud."

"Did you find the safe?"

"Not yet, boss. Everything's kind of spread out around the parking lot. One good thing, though."

"Tell me something good, please."

"My truck's okay. I got away just in time."

"Oh, yeah, that's a big, fat, fucking relief!"

"I'm glad you feel that way, too, boss. Is there anything else you want me to do?"

"Yeah, stick around there and see if you can find the safes. There are two of them. I'll be there in half an hour."

"Right, boss. I'll conduct a search for the safe."

"Safes. Two of them."

"Both of them."

Manny hung up and got into his pants. He was halfway to the site of the ex-trailer when he remembered. Then he called Vinnie.

"Hello?"

"You sound sleepy."

"Is that you, Manny?"

"Yeah, why are you asleep when my trailer is gone?"

"Your trailer? The Airstream?"

"That's the only trailer I got."

"It was stolen?"

"It was exploded."

"Exploded?"

"Like, with a bomb."

"Holy shit."

"I want you to get over to lot five right now and find the safes. They're both missing."

"Manny, I can't get right over there. I'm in New York, have been for several days. Remember?"

"Oh, yeah," Manny said. "How long will it take you to get here?"

"A while, I'm staying the week."

"The fuck you are. Get over there."

"Nothing I can do there. By the time I get a plane, the track and the cops will have taken care of it."

"Vinnie, do what I tell you. Your guy, Fratelli, musta done this."

"Well, I warned you not to try to screw him, Manny. But you got greedy."

"I want you over to the track now!"

"No, thanks. I'm going back to sleep."

"I'll wring your neck."

"Manny? Do you remember who my brother-in-law is?" Pause. "I thought so." Vinnie hung up.

21

Manny knew what the next call had to be, and that he should wait until the Big Guy, Antonio Datilla, had finished breakfast. He waited until ten o'clock. Then just as he reached for the phone, it rang. **Shit!** "Hello?"

"You know who this is."

It was Sal, consigliere to Don Tony. This was bad.

"Sure, I do. I had my hand on the phone to call the Don with some news."

"The Don has already heard the news," Sal said. "All he needs to know now is who and why."

"You remember Johnny Fratelli?"

"Big, scary guy, who took care of Buono in the joint?"

"That's the one."

"He gave Vinnie a mil to spread, for five points a week."

"And?"

"After a while, I figured we had paid him enough, so I stopped the vig."

"What about the principal?"

"Principal?"

"Johnny Fratelli's mil. Did you give that back?"

"Yeah. I figured the Don would give it back to Fratelli, if he thought it was right."

"Well, if he got his mil back, why is he blowing up our trailer?"

"It's complicated."

"Simplify it for me."

"I told Vinnie to get it back. I sent Vinnie to New York to find Fratelli, but he couldn't."

"So Fratelli has kept his money? Why was he annoyed?"

"I guess he didn't want to give it back to me again."

"You know what I would do if you asked me for a mil back?"

"Ah, no."

"I'd blow up your trailer. Okay, Manny, here's what you're going to do: you're going to go down to the Airstream trailer lot on the Dixie Highway, and you're going to purchase a brand-new trailer, a big one, with your own money."

"If that's what the Don wants."

"If I had spoken to the Don about this, you would already be floating, facedown, in Biscayne Bay."

"Okay, sure, glad to oblige."

"And our books show a little under three million in those two safes."

"About that."

"Then you better pray the safes are found, intact, or you can add that to your bill."

"Jesus, Sal, where am I going to raise three mil?"

"Vinnie will loan it to you, at the usual rate."

"I'll find the safes!"

"Good luck. I'll hear from Vinnie about that later today."

"You'll hear from me."

"Nah, you're taking orders from Vinnie, now. He's got your job. And you've got his, hustling down at the track. Tell me you understand me."

"I understand you, Sal."

"You do this right, and the Don won't hear about it. You put a foot wrong, and you're bait." Sal hung up.

Manny hung up, too, and he was sweating heavily.

22

Manny put away his phone and started looking for the two safes. A car pulled up across the lot and sat there. Someone was watching. Manny redoubled his efforts. He found the larger of the two safes, intact, under a bleacher. A few moments later he found the smaller safe, its door ajar. It was half full of hundreds, the rest were lying about it, like fallen leaves. What Manny needed was a rake, but all he had was his hands.

Vinnie was watching Manny from the car when his phone rang. He hoped it was Johnny Fratelli, because he had a few things to say to him

"This is Vinnie."

"You know who this is." It was never a question.

"Sure, good morning."

"What are you doing at this moment?" Sal asked.

"I'm watching Manny on his hands and knees, raking up Franklins. He's doing a pretty good job."

"Here's the way it's going to be," Sal said. "You now have Manny's job, and he has yours. Capisce?"

"I'm not sure I want his job," Vinnie said. "If I had it, I'd be on my hands and knees right now, raking up money, instead of in my box at the track, enjoying the racing."

"You can do the job from your box, for all I care, as long as the count gets done and shipped every day."

"And who will do that job?"

"Manny. He's you now."

"Nah, I'd spend all my time watching my back and watching him try to steal your money. I got no interest."

"Vinnie, it's double what you were making, and Manny is making a third of what he was making."

"That makes him dangerous," Vinnie said. "The job is unattractive with him around."

"Then fire him, put a cap in his head, and he's no more worry."

"You've got people who do that faster and better than I could do," Vinnie said. "My gift is handling money." Vinnie knew that he was edging pretty close to insubordination. And certainly, he would never have said this to the Don himself. But Sal's job was to translate for the Don, then pass down the orders.

"Done. And he'll buy you a new trailer today, too. And replace the three mil in the safes."

"Don't worry about that: the big one was not breached, and he's raking up the money from the little one now."

"Fine. As soon as the new trailer is there and hooked up, tell Manny he's working too hard and to take a few days off. He won't come back."

"I got a kid who's a runner, could do my old job."

"Good. Do it. Pay yourself and him in cash."

"I'll commit for a year," Vinnie said.

"What? It'll take you a year to learn the job."

"I learned it in a week, when I came to work for Manny," Vinnie said.

"Okay, you got yourself a deal. Start by doing whatever you have to to make Johnny Fratelli a happy man."

"I've already done that, and I don't know where he is. If he wants to talk, he calls."

"Smart guy, Johnny." Sal hung up.

Manny got home late, his suit filthy and ruined. He'd never known how hard it was to corral hundred-dollar bills in a breeze, but it was all secured, and there was a new Airstream in lot five, all hooked up. Not that he was happy about it.

"Hilda!" he shouted. He was hungry, and he wanted dinner now.

"Shut your mouth," she called from upstairs. "I'll be down when I'm ready."

This was grounds for severe punishment, but he was too tired to go upstairs and administer it. Then he saw the pile of suitcases in the living room. He walked in there and hefted a couple. All packed.

There was a rap on the door, and two men in workmen's clothes opened the door and walked in. "Outta the way," one of them said to Manny. "We're taking the rest of her stuff."

"The hell you are," Manny said, and he produced enough adrenaline to propel him up the stairs. He stopped at the top and panted a little. He heard the front door close and a truck start up outside.

"Hilda!" he screamed.

Hilda came out of the bedroom, fully dressed and carrying her mink coat on a hanger. "Oh, shut up," she said, producing a silenced pistol from under the coat.

"What the fuck?" Manny said.

"You," she replied. "You're fucked." She shot him in the head, and he collapsed in a heap, then she put another one in his brain. "Compliments of Sal and the Don," she said, then walked downstairs to a waiting car with a driver, who held the door for her.

"All done?" he asked.

"Done," she said.

"Somebody's coming to torch the place," he replied.

"We won't wait," she said. "I've got a plane to catch."

Vinnie was sitting in his new Airstream, tidying his new desk. The two safes had been installed and the toilet charged with the requisite chemicals. There was a pot of coffee on the stove, and the fridge was stocked with beer and diet drinks. His cell phone rang.

"This is Vinnie."

"It's Johnny," he said.

"Speak of the devil," Vinnie said, laughing. "You know who was just asking about you?"

"Who would that be?"

"Sal. He's consigliere now."

"Good for him."

"I'll give you a number, you ever need anything."

Jack wrote it down. "Why would he want to hear from me?"

"He holds you in high regard, the way you

handle things. He asked me to make you happy, if I got a chance."

"I'll pocket that one for a while."

"Oh, I'm sitting here in a brand-new Airstream trailer, not that you would care about that. And I've got Manny's job."

"What happened to Manny?"

"I hear he went on an extended vacation. You ought to see this trailer. It's really something!"

"I'll take your word for it."

"You're happy then?"

"Pretty much."

"Any problems?"

"Just one, but I'll solve that problem eventually."

"Call me if you need something. Or if it's really important, call Sal."

"Give Sal my best." He hung up.

23

Stone and Dino arrived at Patroon in Dino's car, and their appointed drinks awaited them on their table.

"What's new?" Stone asked.

"Not much."

"I thought the NYPD was constantly aboil. Have the criminals taken a vacation?"

"They're working pretty good at Hialeah," Dino said. "Did you see the exploding trailer on TV?" Security camera footage of the explosion had gone viral.

"How could I miss it. And I loved the part with the guy on his hands and knees, raking up C-notes."

"That was Manny Fiore, the mob's big-time bookie down there."

"If he's so big, what's he doing on his hands

and knees? Don't those guys have minions for that sort of work?"

"I guess, where C-notes are involved, they want people they can trust. Still, he's not a worry anymore."

"Did he have an, ah, accident?"

"The kind of accident that gets you two in the head. They found what's left of him a few hours ago, in the ashes of his house. The autopsy turned up two 9mm slugs."

"He must have missed a few hundreds."

"Word has it he's already been replaced by a guy named Vinnie Rossi, who worked for him. Interestingly, somebody recently spotted Vinnie on Fifth Avenue and gave the department a call."

"What interest would the department have in the activities of Hialeah mobsters?"

"We like to know if guys like that come to town. Just between you and me, the FBI has a master list of guys who might be important. If there's a sighting, it goes into the computer."

"Did he blow up the trailer?"

"No indication of that. He worked for the guy who worked in the trailer. The FBI wants to talk to the girl who lived with Manny, name of Hilda Ross, a nightclub singer."

"Nightclub singers still exist?"

"As long as there are nightclubs," Dino said.

"Nightclubs still exist?"

"In Florida, yeah. They can't play golf all the time. Even a few left in New York."

"I don't get it. If the guy is dead, why do they want to talk to the girlfriend?"

"Well, when they went through what was left of his house, they didn't find a single female garment there. Plenty of neckties, etcetera, but no frilly bras and such."

"So she packed up before the house burned?"

"That's the idea."

"This story gets more and more interesting," Stone said.

"It gets more interesting than that," Dino said, handing him the **New York Post,** opened and turned back. A small ad in the corner held a photo of a beautiful woman in a low-cut gown, and a headline read:

RETURN ENGAGEMENT TONIGHT:
HILDA ROSS SINGS JAZZ

"I like the near-absence of the dress," Stone said. "Have you called the FBI?"

"Certainly. You and I are meeting a G-man I know there for the ten o'clock show."

The club was better than Stone had expected: it was roomy and the tables didn't put you elbow-to-elbow with others. The decor was handsome, and when the trio began to play, the sound system was good. They were given a good table, and a moment later a decently dressed FBI agent joined them.

"Stone Barrington, meet Brian Goode," Dino said.

Stone shook his hand. "Good to meet you, no pun intended. I hear you have a fugitive at large in the building."

"Not at large, exactly," Goode said. "There's no warrant. But she's been a confidential informant for nigh onto a year, and I hear she sings well. And we want to talk to her."

Stone leaned near to Dino's ear. "Has he heard about the two slugs in the autopsy?"

"Yes, I've heard about that," Goode said. "And I read lips pretty good."

"Don't fuck with the FBI," Dino said.

"Is she a suspect in the shooting?" Stone asked.

"Not yet," Goode said. "Though we'll have some questions to ask her about that."

The trio finished its number, and a voice over the PA system said, "Ladies and gentlemen, please welcome back Hilda Ross!" The applause was enthusiastic.

The velvet curtains parted and a curvy woman in a tight, green dress with auburn hair followed her impressive cleavage onto the stage, to a waiting microphone.

The group ripped into Rodgers and Hart's "Johnny One-Note," an up-tempo number that gave her an opportunity to use her big voice.

Stone was impressed.

When the set was over Dino said to Stone, "I know, you want to meet her."

"Only if she's innocent of wrongdoing," Stone said.

But Brian Goode was already escorting her to the table and pulling out a chair for her.

"Good evening, gentlemen," she said, shaking each hand and apparently remembering their names.

"That was a great set," Stone said. "I'm a lover of Rodgers and Hart."

"Who isn't?" she asked. "Are you all law enforcement?"

"Just Brian and me," Dino said. "I'm a local. This guy used to be"—he jerked a thumb at Stone—"but the work was too honest for him. Now he's a lawyer."

"Do I need a lawyer, Brian?"

"Everybody needs a lawyer now and then."

"Then you'd better give me your card, Stone."

Stone did so, and she made it disappear somewhere in her cleavage.

She tucked a card of her own into Stone's breast pocket. "I'm in town for a week, maybe two," she said.

"That ought to be long enough," Dino muttered.

"I'll call you when you least expect it," Stone said.

"Then I'll expect the unexpected," she replied.

"Hilda," Brian said, "can we have a little chat at the bar for a minute or two?"

"My time is yours, G-man," she said, and the two of them left the table.

"Very nice," Stone said.

"I thought you would think so."

24

Stone and Hilda left the club immediately after her midnight show.

"Are you worn out after all that work?" Stone asked.

"Hardly," she said. "I'm in shape for it."

"My house is between here and your hotel," he said. "Can I force a nightcap on you?"

"That's an interesting way to put it," she said. "Why not? 'The night is young and you're so beautiful,'" she sang.

"You're not so bad yourself," Stone replied. He bent over and kissed her on the nape of her neck.

"That was nice," she said.

"More?"

"Yes, but let's not start something we can't finish in the back of a cab."

The cab stopped at Stone's house, and they

walked up the front steps. "Nice view," she said, looking up and down the block.

"It's even nicer inside." He let them into the house and walked her through the living room to his study, where he lit a fire and poured them a brandy. She set down her drink, reached up, and helped him off with his jacket.

"Thank you," he said. "Is there anything I can help you off with?"

She made a motion toward her dress. "This is all there is," she said.

Stone reached behind her and pulled the zipper down as far as it would go. The dress fell into a puddle, and she kicked it away.

The sight of her was breathtaking, Stone thought.

She dealt with his belt buckle and the trousers, while he got out of his shirt. Soon he was naked and she, nearly so. He peeled away her thong and sat her down on the sofa, then knelt in front of her and began explorations.

"You know," she said, "if you were a horse, you'd be called a fast starter." He sat down on the sofa, and she took him in her hand. "And there are other equine resemblances," she said.

After that, everything was a blur for the next half hour.

* * *

Finally, they made it upstairs to his bedroom, where they had a shower together.

"Let's take it again from the top," she said. And they did. Sometime during the dark of night it happened again, and nobody complained.

When there was sunlight streaming through the windows, Stone ordered breakfast for them, then took the tray off the dumbwaiter and set it between them. Stone switched on CNN, just in time for a replay of the exploding trailer.

"That was the former office of my former boyfriend," Hilda said.

There was another shot of Manny picking up hundreds that made her laugh. "That is not the sort of work he's accustomed to," she said. "He'd better hope his bosses don't see it."

"I think they probably did see it," Stone said, "resulting in his disappearance."

Hilda swiveled her head. **"What?"**

"I heard about it last night, from Dino. The fed knew, too, didn't he mention it?"

"Has he turned up?"

"He turned up in the smoking ruin of his house, deep fried. An autopsy found two bullets in his head."

"Jesus," she said. "I slept in that house until a couple of days ago."

"Sounds like your timing for leaving was good."

"I hadn't planned it, I just got fed up. He came home while I was moving out, and words were spoken. I was lucky I got out of there without a broken nose."

"Were there witnesses who saw you leave and got a look at him, too?"

"Yes, there were: two guys from the storage place and a cabdriver, who drove me to the airport."

"Don't forget their names or how to get in touch with them."

"Did Brian Goode know about this?"

"I think he was the one who told Dino."

"I wonder why he didn't mention it to me."

"You could put that to him in the form of a question. Oh, and expect to be hearing from the local cops down there."

"Should I be worried?" she asked.

"Not if the three guys cover you. One would be enough, but three is solid gold."

"Whew! I mean, I'm sorry Manny's dead, but not sorry enough to get blamed for it."

"Who hated him enough to do this?"

"How long have you got? He was not a lovable guy most of the time, and burning down the house is just the sort of thing he would have done himself when he was angry—and he was plenty angry the last time I saw him."

"Have you got a cell phone?"

"Yes, but I turned it off when I was performing—ah, singing—last night, and I didn't turn it back on."

"Chances are you have a message or two relating to Manny."

She found her purse and switched on the phone. "You're right," she said, "but I don't feel like talking to them now."

"There's not likely going to be a time when you'll feel like talking to the police about somebody who's been murdered, so don't put it off. It will just get harder."

"Then I may as well suck it up," she said. "Excuse me for a while." She went into the bathroom and closed the door behind her.

Stone was halfway through the **Times** crossword before she emerged again, this time wearing her dress and brushing her hair.

"How'd it go?"

"Okay, I think, but you never know about those guys."

"Did they read you your rights?"

She looked at him. "No. Should they have?"

"They should have. You may want to remember that later, if they come back."

"Are they likely to?"

"It's almost guaranteed."

"What should I say to them then?"

"Say, 'Gentlemen, I've told you everything I know about these events, and I will have nothing further to say about them.' Then hang up. If they keep trying, call me before you talk to them again."

She sat down on the bed and kissed him. "You're a dear, not to mention terrific in the hay."

"Another horse reference," Stone said.

"Now, I've got to go to my hotel and put on some civilian clothes. I have an appointment with a record producer for lunch."

"Don't get stuck with the tab," Stone said, kissing her goodbye. "My driver will meet you downstairs and drive you to your hotel. If you like, he'll wait and drive you to lunch, too."

"Oh, how nice!"

"His name is Fred. If you encounter a Labrador retriever on the way out, his name is Bob—so you won't confuse them."

She gave him another kiss, then left.

Stone called Fred and gave him his instructions.

25

Stone took a call from Dino later that morning.

"Hey."

"Has she cleared the premises yet?"

"Who? What premises?"

"Guess who, and which premises."

"Oh, you mean Hilda?"

"That's right. She has a name."

"She does. Feel free to use it when speaking of her."

"You sound a little defensive," Dino said. "That means she stayed the night, huh?"

"It was late when she finished her second set. I wouldn't put a young woman out in the street in the dead of night."

"Not if you could put her to bed instead," Dino said.

"Why are you giving me a hard time about Hilda?"

"Because you don't know what you're getting into."

"I believe I do. I've traversed that terrain before, and I've never regretted it."

"Well, let's hope she'll be allowed conjugal visits at Bedford Hills Women's Prison."

"Why would she have any need to? She can just come here. By the way, 'conjugal' refers to her marital status. I never sleep with married women. Not on purpose, anyway."

"I know at least three married women you've slept with."

"Well, accidents will happen."

"The Bureau thinks Hilda's a contract killer."

"Yeah? Who, exactly, at the Bureau?"

"Brian Goode."

"All by himself, I expect."

"I trust his judgment," Dino said.

"But not mine."

"I have more experience with yours."

"So you trust the word of a boy wonder G-man, instead of your friend and partner of lo these many years."

"Former partner."

"I'm smarter now than I was then," Stone said.

"I could buy that, if you weren't sleeping with a contract killer."

"That is an unsubstantiated characterization."

"The Florida cops think she's a contract killer, too."

"So, we have to take the word of out-of-state cops to make good judgments?"

"Only when they're right. Have they contacted her yet?"

"This morning."

"What did she tell them?"

"Nothing they didn't already know from her previous statement."

"Did they read her her rights?"

"Not yet. I've told her that if they contact her again, she should say that she has nothing to add to her previous statement, and that she won't address the issue again without the presence of her attorney."

"Sounds like she's talked to a lawyer."

"I was conveniently located."

"Stone, why, in the face of all the evidence, do you refuse to believe that she's a hit person?"

"All **what** evidence?"

"Well . . ."

"Aha! There isn't any, is there?"

"There's no evidence to the contrary, either."

"Wrong. She has three witnesses who saw her leave the house with Manny Fiore still alive inside."

"And who would they be?"

"The two moving men who carted her stuff to storage, and the cabdriver who took her to the airport."

"That's their opinion?"

"It's a fact, not an opinion. And who does your G-man and the Florida cops think set the house on fire after they left?"

"An arsonist."

"Good guess!" Stone cried.

"A professional arsonist. One of those people Jimmy Breslin used to say earns their living by 'building vacant lots.'"

"And when did this putative arsonist go to work?"

"He chose an appropriate moment."

"Try telling that to a jury sometime. They'll acquit before the coffee has dried on your upper lip."

Dino licked his lips. "All right," he said, "I'll await further developments before I make up my mind on her guilt or innocence."

Stone held up a cautionary finger. "I never said she was innocent."

"She's either guilty or innocent," Dino said.

"Not necessarily. There's an area in between."

"What area?"

"Ah . . . **knowing**. That's it, she's knowing."

"That must come in handy."

"What else would you expect of a bright young woman?"

"Guilt or innocence?"

"Then once again, I choose innocence."

"Okay, I'm outta here," Dino said, then hung up.

* * *

Joan came in and placed an envelope on his desk. "I found this on your desk this morning," she said. "It appears to have been there about ten days, unopened."

Stone opened the envelope and found an invitation to dinner at the home of Jack and Hillary Coulter. For that evening.

"What? This is for tonight?"

"I wouldn't know," Joan said, being innocent of any contact with it.

Stone quickly dialed the number.

"The Coulter residence," a butler intoned.

"This is Stone Barrington. May I speak with either one, please?"

"One moment, Mr. Barrington," he said.

A moment later, Hillary came on the line. "Stone?"

"Yes, Hillary. My secretary has just handed me, unopened, your very kind invitation to dinner this evening."

"Bad secretary," Hillary replied, in the manner of speaking to a dog.

"I do apologize for her, and I'd be happy to come, if the invitation is still open. I perfectly understand if you've asked someone else."

"Nonsense," she said. "We'll see you at seven for drinks. I suppose you have a date?"

"Yes, I do. Her name is Hilda Ross."

"Noted. See you then." She hung up.

Joan came back into the room. "I suppose you blamed me."

"Of course, I did," Stone replied, dialing Hilda's number.

"Hallo, dahlink," Hilda said, in a broad Hungarian accent.

"Good news," Stone said. "We've had a great dinner invitation. Joan gave it to me ten minutes ago, unopened. It's for tonight. I hope you're up for it, because I've already accepted for both of us."

"In that case, I accept, too. How are we dressing?"

"Black tie."

"Then I'll wear a work dress. They're the nicest things I have with me."

"I'm sure I'll love it. All the gentlemen will, too, if not necessarily all the ladies."

"I'm accustomed to that," she said.

"We're due at seven for drinks."

"What? That only gives me eight hours to get ready!"

"You'll manage." Stone hung up. "You are forgiven," he said to Joan.

26

They were on their way to the Coulters' Fifth Avenue apartment for drinks and dinner.

"Who are the Coulters?" Hilda asked.

"Just a very nice Fifth Avenue couple who also live in Palm Beach and Northeast Harbor, Maine, depending on which way the wind blows."

"What does he do?"

"He's retired from being an investment adviser, I think," Stone said. No point going into Jack's early criminal life and prison term.

"And she?"

"Hillary? Her family company was recently sold."

"Don't you know any people who work for a living?"

"Well, let's see: There's you. Then there's Dino. Then there's just about everybody else I know. Do you think all my friends are shiftless?"

"How many will we be for dinner?"

"Could be eight, could be eighty. It's a big apartment, and they like entertaining."

They were deposited on the sidewalk, as the doorman held first the car door, then the building door open for them. In the elevator, Stone pressed the button marked PH. The car rose swiftly. The door opened into the apartment's foyer, then they walked down a curving flight of stairs and into the living room, which contained nearer to eighty than eight guests.

"Good guess on the numbers," Hilda said. "God, I'm glad I wore my good jewelry."

They snagged glasses of champagne from a passing waiter, and Stone showed her the terrace. "If you'd been with me the last time I was here, you'd have wished you hadn't worn your good jewelry."

"Why?"

"Well, at about this point in the evening, I was standing out here, chatting with my date, when out of the corner of my eye, I saw a man dressed in black clothes and a black hood in the living room, and he was carrying a shotgun."

"What was it, a costume party?"

"Not in the least. Turned out the man had three friends, each with his own black outfit and shotgun, and they went about the room relieving the guests of the burden of their jewelry."

"What did you do?"

"Well, I told my date to remove all her jewelry and give it to me, and I put it in my coat pocket."

"Didn't she think that odd?"

"I expect so, but I think there was enough urgency in my voice to make her think I was serious. Then I kissed her."

"Why?"

"Well, first of all, she was very kissable. Second, I thought it would distract the robbers, when they got around to us."

"Did it?"

"Only momentarily, then they asked for her jewelry. She smartly said, 'I don't wear jewelry,' then I explained that I had only a wristwatch, and it had my name engraved on the back and possession of it might cost him a prison term, so he went away and left us alone on the terrace."

"So her jewelry didn't get stolen?"

"No, they never frisked me."

"What happened after that?"

"Well, I gave her jewelry back, then the police were called, dinner was served, I think in that order. All of the jewelry was recovered when the police arrested one of the robbers the next day."

They were interrupted by Jack Coulter, and Stone introduced them. Jack seemed to take a great interest in her, it seemed to Stone.

Later, when Hilda was visiting the powder

room, Jack took Stone aside. "How long have you known Hilda?" he asked.

"Only a few days. Why do you ask?"

"I once knew her father very well."

"Where and how?"

"At what was my upstate residence, at the time. Joe Rossetti, his name was, and we had adjoining suites. He had the better river view, though. I used to see Hilda, who was in her teens, when she came on visitors' days, to see her father."

"What was he in for?"

"Robbery. But Joe was known to be mobbed up, and he had a reputation for the high quality of his work."

"As a robber?"

"As a hitman. He got out sooner than I did. Last I heard, he was retired, living in Florida somewhere."

"When she comes back, don't bring up her father," Stone said. "I'll tell you why some other time."

"As you wish," Jack said.

Hilda returned. "You two look as if you've been telling each other dirty jokes," she said reprovingly.

"Not a bit of it," Stone said. "You were a long time in the powder room."

"On the way back I ran into somebody I knew, and we had a chat."

"Who was that?" Jack asked.

"Forrest, your pianist. We've worked together a few times."

"Hilda is a singer," Stone said. "Fortunately, this is her night off."

"Perhaps you'll sing something for us after dinner," Jack said.

"Of course. I'd be happy to."

Jack excused himself.

"Does that happen a lot?" Stone asked.

She shrugged. "Now and then. I'm happy to oblige."

They got another drink and sat on the terrace. "Where did you grow up?" he asked

"In Florida," she replied.

"Where?"

"Always near a racetrack. My father was an inveterate player of the ponies. He did well at it, too; supported the family. There were times when it seemed he was getting a winner or two a week."

"He must have been a hell of a handicapper," Stone said, and let the subject drop. He knew next to nothing about horse racing.

After dinner, Jack introduced Hilda, and she sang two Cole Porter numbers for them, then sat down to much applause.

"Thank you," Stone said. "It's always nice to

have a date who can earn her dinner. Hillary and Jack will always ask you back now."

"What a good idea," she said.

On the way home afterward, Stone nearly asked about her father, but stopped himself. Maybe she really did think he had earned his living as a handicapper.

27

Vinnie sat in his luxurious new trailer and watched his assistant, Maria, count the money. She could count a hundred grand in hundreds in a flash; her fingers flew, and Vinnie could never keep track, but she didn't make mistakes. It took a couple of days before Vinnie caught on. The reason Manny had loved his job so much was that Maria did all the work, while he watched old movies on satellite TV and occasionally ambled down to the track and watched a few races run, just so he wouldn't forget what a horse looked like.

What's more, Vinnie was making nearly three times what he had in his old job. On his third day on the job, he gave Maria a big raise and got her to promise not to retire while he was still alive.

Maria was a pretty, quite buxom woman who hadn't gained a pound since she was sixteen. It didn't take Vinnie long to discover that she had a keen interest in sex. Apparently, her husband had forgotten how, and after all, she was entitled to a sex life, wasn't she? He took it upon himself to see that she got the attention she craved, and she craved him, too. If he had known about this, he would have knocked off Manny years before.

It was obvious to Vinnie that Manny had not taken retirement and run off to an island somewhere, and his suspicions were confirmed when Manny's house burned down with him in it. The medical examiner had taken one look at his remains and diagnosed lead poisoning.

Those were the rules of the game, Vinnie figured: you pissed off somebody higher up the ladder than you, and you got your brains scrambled. Vinnie tried never to piss off anybody.

Stone and Hilda were having lunch at La Goulue, in the East Sixties.

"How long have you known Jack Coulter?" Hilda asked.

"I don't know, a while. A client who was a friend of his recommended him to me."

"He reminds me of somebody I once knew," she said, "but I can't place him. What do you do for Jack, exactly?"

"Jack is one of those clients who has the whole

firm of Woodman & Weld at his disposal: He wants to buy a house somewhere, we find him a Realtor to write the offer and close the sale. He gets himself a new wife and wants his will rewritten, it's done. He's looking at an investment and wants the seller investigated, the man is gone over with a fine-tooth comb, and so is the deal. Why does Jack interest you?" He thought it better to encourage this than to appear to be withholding information.

"As I said, he looks familiar, something about the way he moves around, the broad shoulders. Not the face, though. Maybe somebody my father knew: Does he spend time in Florida?"

"I told you: Palm Beach. He and Hillary have a big apartment at the Breakers."

"My father wouldn't know anybody at the Breakers, unless he was collecting a debt for a bookie."

"Your father did that sort of work?"

"He was a sort of Jack-of-all-trades, I guess you'd say. Somebody wanted something done, my dad saw to it."

"Was he mobbed up?"

"He certainly knew people in that milieu," she said, "but he wasn't a member of anything."

"A freelancer then."

"Exactly."

Stone took a deep breath. "Did he teach you things?"

"He taught me to play every card game available and showed me what a fast horse looks like. That was about it."

Stone exhaled. He didn't want to be seen shying away from her background, but he wanted to know about it anyway. He changed the subject. After all, she wasn't going to tell him how her father had taught her to shoot people in the head, not just once, but twice.

After lunch, he turned Hilda loose in Bloomingdale's with a credit card, then went home. Dino was waiting for him, and he almost never dropped by the house in the daytime. Something was up.

"Is it too early for Scotch?" he asked Dino.

"It's five o'clock somewhere," Dino replied.

Stone handed him the drink.

"You're not having something?"

"I had wine with lunch. I don't want to sleep the afternoon away." Dino wanted to tell him something; he could feel it.

"So, what's new?" Stone asked, nudging him a little.

"Not much. Oh, I did hear something interesting, but it's just a rumor. I can't prove it."

"Oh?"

"It's about Hilda."

Stone nodded. "Sure, it is."

"Do you know what her father did for a living?"

"Funny, we just had a conversation about that over lunch. He handicapped horses and did odd jobs for the boys."

"What sort of jobs?"

"Debt collection, that sort of thing. He wasn't mobbed up, he was just a resource for them, near as I could tell."

"A resource, huh."

"Sort of like that, I think."

"I heard something a little more definite," Dino said.

"Well, you have big ears, Dino. Come on, spit it out."

"I heard he was what you might call a 'sought-after' hitman."

"Really?"

"You think Hilda knew about that?"

"You think she'd tell me if she did?"

"Maybe not."

"It's not the sort of things she'd tell the kids at school, is it?"

"I guess not."

"Then why would she tell me? Would she think that would impress me?"

"I guess not."

"I'm willing to believe that's true, Dino. What I'm not willing to believe is that being a hired killer is the sort of thing a father passes down to his daughter."

"How about if Dad got sick, or was just old and feeble and couldn't earn anymore?"

"Is that what you heard?"

"It was intimated."

"That would make it understandable," Stone said. "But that doesn't mean I want to hear it."

"Wouldn't you rather know the truth than not know?"

"No, Dino, I would not. And I'd appreciate it if you'd keep that in mind."

"I'll try to do that," Dino said. He knocked back his Scotch and left.

Stone felt a little unsettled, in spite of himself.

28

Stone glanced at his watched, just as his phone rang: 5:00.

"Hello?"

"It's Hilda."

"You all shopped out?"

"Pretty much. I just got a call. I've got to go home. My daddy's sick, and it looks bad."

"I'm sorry to hear it. You want Fred to drive you to the airport?"

"The hotel is putting my luggage in a cab as we speak."

"Call me when you get in, to let me know you made it all right."

"Okay."

"Are you staying at your father's?"

"Probably."

"Want to give me a number there?"

"No. Daddy talks only on throwaway cells. You've got my number, if you need to reach me."

"Sure. Are you ever coming back?"

"It depends on Daddy and work. Most of my work is in Florida. I get a job in New York only occasionally."

"You don't need a job to come see me."

"I know that, baby, and I'm going to miss you. Bye, now. Gotta run."

"Bye bye."

She hung up.

Stone suddenly remembered that she had some clothes upstairs in the guest dressing room. He called her cell to ask where he could send them, and got a recorded message: **The number you have called is not in service at this time.**

He was sure he had called her on her cell phone at some point, but he couldn't remember when. Hilda was gone—**poof**—and he didn't know where. He'd keep his dinner date without her. Dino was going to love this.

The after-office crowd at P. J. Clarke's was at its peak when Stone arrived. Dino wasn't there yet, so Stone squeezed himself into a spot at the bar and raised his chin toward the bartender, who already had his hand on the Knob Creek bottle.

"You have a broad back," a female voice said from behind him. "Is there a face at the top of it?"

He turned around for a glimpse of his neighbor, then turned all the way around. "Will this do?" he asked pointing a finger at his head.

She was tall, slender, and had a lot of dark, wavy hair. If she had a brain, then she was about all Stone required of a woman. She was wearing an expensive-looking black mink coat. "I suppose it will have to do," she said, "if that's all you've got."

"It's the best I can manage on short notice," Stone said. "What is your name, if I may ask?"

"You may," she replied. "I'm Tara Wilkes."

"Great-granddaughter of Ashley Wilkes? Do I detect what's left of a Southern accent?"

"If you have sharp ears."

"And I suppose your mother was a **Gone With the Wind** freak."

"An accurate supposition. You'd be surprised how few notice the name at first bite."

"Nobody reads thousand-page novels anymore."

"I don't know," she said, "it still sells a zillion copies a year."

"I wouldn't be surprised. Apart from your name, do you share any other features of the novel?"

"Well, I'm nicer than Melanie's sister-in-law, India, but not as nice as Melanie."

"That's all right. Nobody is as nice as Melanie."

"You know," she said, "I think we're somewhere past the point where courtesy dictates that you tell me your name."

"I apologize for all my shortcomings," Stone said.

"That's Rhett's line."

"I apologize for my discourtesy and my lack of attribution. My name is Stone Barrington."

"That sounds almost pretentious. Is it from a novel?"

"Not from one I've read or ever heard of. Stone is from my mother's family and Barrington from my father's."

"Then it's honestly come by, unlike mine, which my grandmother thought was cheap."

"You're lucky your mother didn't call you 'Scarlett.'"

"That would have been too cheap, even for my mother."

Dino pushed his way to the bar behind Tara. "Don't mind me," he said to her.

She looked down at him. "Does it matter if I do?"

"Really," Stone said, "don't mind him. He's with me."

"He's your **date**?" she asked.

"In a manner of speaking, but only that. However, I'm flattered that you think I could do better. Tara, this is Dino Bacchetti. Dino's wife travels a lot, either on business or to get away from him, or both, and I have to buy him dinner when she's gone or he would starve to death."

"Well, I suppose you two are going to dine now."

"We were hoping—at least I was—that you'd dine with us. You're so much more attractive than Dino."

"I accept your judgment and your invitation," she said.

They were working their way through the crowd toward the dining room at the rear, when Dino asked, sotto voce, "Where's Hilda?"

"She had to go back to Florida, a sick father."

"What time did she fly out?"

"Sometime after five," Stone said. "That's when she called."

"Interesting," Dino said.

"What?"

"You know the bookie, Tiny Blanco?"

"I've seen him at a clam house downtown."

"Funny you should mention that," Dino said. "That's where he got wiped this afternoon, around three o'clock." He paused for effect. "Two in the head."

29

They were given a corner table, with Tara Wilkes between them.

"What's good?" she asked, reading the menu off the wall.

"Whatever sounds good," Stone said, "the beef, particularly."

They all ordered strip steaks, and Stone ordered a good cabernet.

"I'm sorry if Stone's a little quiet," Dino said to Tara. "He just got some bad news."

"Ignore him," Stone said. "It's just bad news in Dino's head."

"Did I mention that the shooter was a woman?" Dino asked.

"Why would you? It's irrelevant."

"If you say so."

"'Shooter'?" Tara asked. "Was somebody shot?"

"A bookie named Tiny, down in Little Italy," Dino replied. "You didn't know him, did you?"

"Dino," Stone said, "I'm about to spill a lot of wine on you. You'll have to pay Madame Paulette a fortune to get the stains out."

"I'm sorry," Dino said, holding up both hands in surrender. "Not a fit discussion over dinner."

Tara looked at Stone. "How is that bad news for you?"

"It isn't. In fact, I think the world is a better place without him. Gamblers everywhere are rejoicing."

"Are you a gambler, Stone?" she asked.

"Not even on sure things," he replied. "Especially not on sure things."

"A man after my own heart," she said.

"My experience with gambling is that I go to a casino with Dino, buy a hundred bucks' worth of chips, then I put them on a table, and somebody takes them away. Where's the fun in that?"

"Stone is not lying about his skills as a gambler," Dino said. "Anything else, well . . ." He waggled a hand back and forth.

"Are you a liar, Stone?" Tara asked.

"Only when paying Dino compliments," Stone said. "Dino, didn't I hear your phone ringing? The one you always have to answer, then go see about something?"

"I didn't hear anything," Dino said innocently.

"Dino is a police officer," Stone said to Tara. "His hearing is a little on the selective side."

"You two are a riot."

"That's what everybody says," Dino chimed in.

"Dino's work is what makes him so entertaining, with lines like 'two in the head.' It's one of his best. Where are you from, Tara?"

"I'm from a small town in Georgia called Delano."

"I've heard of that," Dino said. "What do you do, Tara?"

"I design handbags," she said.

"I'll bet you've got a huge wardrobe," Dino said.

"Well, I've got a lot of handbags."

"You deserved that, Dino," Stone said.

"Do you have a brand name?" Dino asked.

"Yes. 'Tara.'"

Stone burst out laughing.

"I know that name," Dino said. "My wife has some handbags with that name on them."

"Well, let me know when her next birthday is, and I'll give you a deal on something in alligator. That's my specialty." She produced cards and handed one to each of them. They responded in kind.

"My goodness," Tara said, reading Dino's. "You **are** a policeman, aren't you? You're the commissioner!"

"I cannot deny it."

"As I said, his work is the source of all his brilliant dinner-table conversation," Stone said. "Any gory sex crimes today, Dino?"

"Nothing good enough for the dinner table."

"What a disappointment," Stone said.

"Are you two sure you're not married?" Tara asked.

"You're not the first to ask," Stone said. "If we were, we'd be divorced."

"Well, if you keep up this banter I'm going to have to spank one of you and send him to bed early," Tara said, reprovingly.

They both raised their hands, and she finally laughed.

After dinner they made their way to the street.

"We both have cars," Stone said. "Can one of us offer you a ride home?"

"Mine has a siren," Dino said. "If you're good, I'll let you turn it on."

"You don't have to be good in my car," Stone said, as the Bentley pulled up to the curb.

"This one looks nice," Tara said. "Thanks anyway, Dino. Maybe another time."

Stone got in beside her. "Where do you live?" he asked.

"Bucks County, Pennsylvania," she replied.

30

Tara was only kidding. She lived in the West Thirties, in Hell's Kitchen. "Sometimes, it **seems** like it's all the way to Bucks County," she explained.

"My house is closer," Stone said. "Why don't we save you the trip to Bucks County?"

"Well, that's blunt," she said.

"It wasn't intended to be." He kissed her lightly. "It was meant to be affectionate."

"Funny how a good steak and a bottle of wine can make you affectionate," she said, kissing him back. "I don't usually do this, but all right."

"'All right' is good enough for me," Stone said. "Home, Fred."

They had cognac in Stone's study.

"This must be a staging area," Tara said.

"Think of it as a springboard," Stone said, leading her to the elevator.

"Too long a climb, is it?" she asked.

"I have to conserve my strength."

"Good idea," she said, and he led her into the bedroom. Undressing didn't take long.

The sun woke them early, and they took the opportunity.

"Would you like some breakfast?" Stone asked afterward.

"Thank you. Whatever you're having."

Stone called down for breakfast. They had just finished making love again when the dumbwaiter chime rang. Stone took the trays to the bed and used the remote controls to sit them up.

"I have to say," Tara said, "I made the right decision last night."

"I'm glad you think so."

"I mean, I thought I'd get a cup of bad coffee, then be cast into the street."

"Fred will drive you home or to work, or both, whenever you like."

"I have a studio in my house," she said, "and a showroom, too."

"Sounds like a big house."

"Not as big as yours. I live on the top two

floors and deduct the bottom two from my taxes."

"I work on the ground floor, in what was a dentist's office when I inherited the house."

"Nice inheritance."

"She was a nice great-aunt," Stone said. "I hold her in fond remembrance."

"Were you ever married?" Tara asked.

"I'm widowed."

"Kids?"

"A son, who lives in California now."

"What does he do out there?"

"He writes and directs films at Centurion Studios. His partner, Ben, who is Dino's son, runs the studio."

Stone showed her where her dressing room and bath were, and she showered and dressed. "That was refreshing," she said. "Nice dressing room. Not a shred of another woman's clothing visible."

"The staff has standing orders to donate any stray garments to Goodwill."

"I plan to leave fully clothed," she said. "The girls in my workshop don't mind if I wear the same thing on successive days."

"What took you across town last night?"

"A failed trip to Bloomie's. I had hoped to find a thing or two and didn't, so I went to P.J.'s to console myself with Scotch."

"I'm so glad you did. May I call you again, soon?"

"You'd damned well better!"

Stone called Fred, and she kissed him and left.

Stone's cell rang. "Good morning, Dino."

"I'm sure I didn't wake you. Has she left already?"

"I'm sure I don't know to whom you're referring."

"Yeah, sure. You said Hilda left for Florida yesterday afternoon?"

"Sometime after five. Why are you interested?"

"I got curious, so I had somebody check the airlines. Nobody by either name—Hilda or Ross—flew to anywhere in Florida after five yesterday."

"You've got this bone in your teeth, and you're not going to let it go, are you?"

"Well, I don't mind her running loose around Florida, but yesterday she made the error of committing first-degree murder on my turf. I don't let go of that. Ever."

"So, I have to hear about it forever?"

"No, just until the DA gets a confession or a conviction."

"You forgot something."

"What's that?"

"The DA isn't stupid enough to charge her on

the evidence you have. Oh, wait a minute. You don't have any evidence, do you?"

"I have a nose," Dino said. "The nose knows."

"You should spend less time listening to your nose, which is sort of an impossibility anyway, and exercise your other senses, dull as they may be."

"I hope you're not in love with her," Dino said. "That would make it harder for me to bust her."

"I am not, but I remain fond of her."

"But you're fond of Tara, too, aren't you? Hasn't she replaced Hilda in your affections?"

"You're just jealous because Tara didn't want to play with your siren last night. That must have stung. Say, is your wife home yet? I miss Viv."

"Then you can join us for dinner tonight, seven at Caravaggio."

"Will do." Stone hung up, found Tara's card, and called her.

"Yesss?"

"Is it too soon to ask you out to dinner again?"

"Certainly not."

"We're dining with Dino and his wife, Vivian—called Viv. I'll pick you up at six-forty-five, if the address on your card is correct."

"I gave you the correct card. I have another one with a bad address and phone number, for jerks, of which I seem to meet too many. Where are we going?"

"To Caravaggio, an Italian joint on the Upper East Side. I'm afraid you'll have to enter that neighborhood again."

"I'll bring my passport," she said. "Gotta run."

She hung up, leaving Stone all warm and funny inside.

31

They were ushered to a deep corner of the dining room, where Dino and Viv awaited them. Dino looked as if he was bursting to tell Stone something, but he contained himself until everybody had a drink before them.

"Did you notice who you walked right by on the way in?" Dino asked, finally.

Stone, who was facing the front of the room, checked out the tables they had passed on the way in. "The older guy with the heroic nose," Stone said. "Who he?"

"He be Antonio Datilla," Dino said.

"The Don?"

"The actual Don. Hisself."

"And the other guy?"

"Sal Trafficante, his consigliere. He's known as the Don's brain."

"I've heard of him."

"Not the first time I've seen him here," Dino said.

"I see two guys in suits, across the aisle from the Don's table," Stone said. "Two guys who look like they're unaccustomed to wearing suits."

"They would be the Don's version of the Secret Service."

"Hence the bulges under their jackets."

"I wish, just once, somebody would try to stop by the Don's table and say hello," Dino said. "I'd like to see those two spring into action."

"Then why don't you stop by on your way out and check their response time."

"I would, if I thought they knew I'm the police commissioner," Dino said. "If they didn't recognize me, I might catch a couple of rounds."

"Don't you go anywhere near that table, Dino," Viv said firmly.

"I'm just speculating," Dino said.

"If you do, I'll take you outside and beat you up. Your guys would never try to stop me."

"Speaking of your guys, Dino," Stone said. "Where are they?"

"They're standing around outside, smoking cigarettes and waiting for something terrible to happen."

"You stole that line," Stone said. "It's from Alex Atkinson's article on Spain, in the September 1963 issue of **Holiday** magazine.

I think he was referring to Franco's Guardia Civil. I remember, because I gave you the piece to read."

"Whatever," Dino said

"Come on, Stone," Viv said. "Who remembers stuff like that from September 1963?"

"There's a tiny corner of my brain that involuntarily stores that sort of information," Stone said. "Nothing I can do about it."

Tara was laughing into her Scotch. "You people know each other too well," she said.

"The paella looks good," Viv said.

"In that same article," Stone said, "Atkinson says he once ate a paella in Valencia that almost certainly contained the left forefinger of a rubber glove."

"I'm skipping the paella," Tara said. "What else is good?"

"If it's on the menu, it's good," Dino said.

"I'll have the paella," Stone said to the hovering captain. "I want to see what I can find in it."

"Lotsa stuff," the captain replied smoothly.

Tara ordered fish, the Bacchettis ordered the paella, and Stone chose a big white Burgundy to accompany everything.

It was around eight-thirty before they considered the dessert menu. Stone noted that the Don and his consigliere were on about the same schedule, and the two of them were on their second bottle of wine.

"I didn't know Mafiosi came to restaurants like this one," Tara said. "I always think of them dining in dimly lit clam houses."

"No," Dino corrected her. "Dimly lit clam houses are where they **shoot** each other."

"I stand corrected," she replied. "I'm glad they're not doing it here."

"The night is young," Dino said.

Then a woman entered a corner of Stone's vision, wearing a fur coat. She shucked it off and gave it to the coat-check woman, revealing a low-cut green dress Stone had seen somewhere before.

Dino had seen her, too. He beckoned the captain and waved him close to his ear. "Who's the lady with the cleavage, dining with the Don?"

"I forget her name," the captain said, "but I know she's a singer, because she's appearing at the Café Carlyle, around the corner. She has another show at ten."

The consigliere stood to greet her, but not the Don. He allowed himself to be pecked on the cheek, then waved her to a chair. Someone brought her a glass of champagne, and she ordered a dessert.

"Why are you two staring?" Viv asked. "Anybody we know?"

"Vaguely," Stone said.

"Vaguely, my ass," Dino chipped in.

"I'm trying very hard not to turn around and look," Tara said.

"Don't worry," Viv replied. "You'll catch her on our way out."

"I wouldn't miss it for the world," Tara said, "after that table-wide reaction."

"Her name is Hilda Ross," Stone said, "née Rossetti. The captain was right; she's a singer."

"Stone knows her better than he should," Dino remarked.

They finished dessert and coffee, and Stone paid the bill. Then they all got up and started for the street. Stone looked ahead; the Don and his consigliere were seated side by side on the banquette, Hilda was on the other side of the table, facing away from Stone.

As they passed the table, the Don took no notice at all: he paid people to do that. However, Trafficante, the consigliere, locked eyes with Stone for about three seconds as his party made their way toward the front door. It was a steady gaze and cool, but there was something else in it that Stone did not like. It was no more than a flicker at the corner of his mouth, but it spoke to Stone of hatred. From a man he had never seen before tonight. It was unsettling.

Hilda never noticed their passing.

As they were getting into the car, Tara said, "Who is the singer—what's her name?"

"Hilda Ross."

"Why is she so interesting?"

"She's supposed to be in another state," Stone replied. Tara didn't bring it up again.

32

Once in the car, Tara said, "I'd better go straight home. I've got a big day tomorrow: buyers coming in from Atlanta and Dallas."

"Of course," Stone muttered. "Fred, would you drop me at home, then take Ms. Wilkes to Bucks County, Pennsylvania?"

There was a perfunctory good-night kiss, and she was gone. Forever, Stone reckoned.

Stone had finished his breakfast and was working on the **Times** crossword, with **Morning Joe** on the TV, when Dino called.

"What the fuck was that about last night?" Stone asked pleasantly.

"What are you talking about? I didn't do anything."

"You certainly blew Tara out of my life. She hardly spoke to me on the way home."

"Then I take it she's not breakfasting with you?"

"You made absolutely certain of that."

"Viv made me do it," Dino said, lamely.

"So you admit it! And the hell Viv made you. You were seething malice!"

"It wasn't as bad as that."

"It was worse. Now Tara thinks I've been going out with some gun moll."

"Looks like she never left the city, doesn't it?" Dino said. "Did you call her while she was still here?"

"I tried."

"Let me guess: **The number you have dialed is out of service.**"

"She uses throwaways."

"Something I'll bet she learned from Joe Rossetti. He's still going strong, you know. I'll bet he was waiting at the Café Carlyle for her ten o'clock show to start. I did a little research on him. He's at the track most days, and the only person he speaks to on the phone is his employer—or rather, his employer's consigliere. What was it with you and Sal Trafficante? I saw that look on the way out."

"I don't know. I've never clapped eyes on the man before."

"Well, he certainly clapped eyes on you, and

who can blame him? You've been screwing one of his employees."

"You don't know that she works for him."

"All right, so you've been screwing his girlfriend, the singer. It hardly matters which."

"Where is Trafficante based?"

"The Don moves around. He has a place in Manhattan, and Sal lives right next door. You know, I'm fascinated by that look he gave you. People he looks at like that usually end up doing a midnight tap dance in the East River, wearing concrete tap shoes."

"You have a rich fantasy life, Dino. You should be writing novels."

"You know I'm right about Hilda Ross, Stone. We learn a little more every day, and it's all bad. You should try and stay on her good side. Maybe she can keep you alive for a few more days."

"Why would anybody want to kill me?" Stone asked plaintively.

"How about jealousy? A famous motive, jealousy. Comes right behind money on Roget's **List of Motives**. That was a jealous look Sal gave you."

"If I keep listening to this I'm going to lose my breakfast."

"You're going to lose a lot more than that, unless you listen harder. Never mind your breakfast."

"I can't talk anymore." Stone hung up. He hadn't been kidding about losing his breakfast;

he was fighting to hold on to it. He wanted to call Hilda and demand an explanation as to why she wasn't in Florida, but he didn't have her number or her e-mail address.

Dino called back.

"What?"

"I was right."

"Right about what?"

"Joe Rossetti was at a ringside table at the Café Carlyle for the ten o'clock show. I called a guy I know there, and he filled me in. The old man has a suite there, too, which he shares with his daughter. And by the way, Hilda's appearance at the Café was booked eight weeks ago."

"All right, so she's a liar," Stone admitted.

"When she calls you, and she will, don't take the call."

"I won't."

"And if you do take the call, don't agree to see her."

"I won't."

"And if you do see her, have Fred pick her up and take her somewhere to meet you. You might also ask Fred to frisk her for weapons—guns, knives, ice picks."

"Dino, I can't take any more of this."

"Dinner at Patroon, eight-thirty?"

"Okay." Stone hung up.

33

Stone was cleaning up his desk after his day when Joan rang.

"Yes?"

"Hilda Ross on one for you."

"Tell her I'm on a conference call. And ask her for a number, one that works, and I'll call her back in a few minutes."

After a moment, the light on the phone went out. Joan came back. "She says she'll call you."

Stone continued to rearrange his desk for another half hour. "The hell with her," he said, finally. Then his cell phone rang.

"Stone Barrington."

"Hi, it's Hilda."

"Hi, there. Sorry I couldn't talk before."

"That's all right. Listen, about last night."

"How did your appearance at the Carlyle go? I'll bet your dad enjoyed it."

That stopped her for a count of about four. "I guess I have some explaining to do," she said finally.

"One thing about explaining," Stone said. "You never have to do it, if you don't lie."

"If I could tell you everything—but I can't—you'd understand why I lied."

"You don't have to tell me anything you don't want to," he said, "but when you want to, then I'd appreciate either the truth or silence."

"That's fair enough, I guess."

"Anything you want to tell me now? I'm listening."

"I didn't expect to see you at Caravaggio last night."

"Nor I, you."

"I got the Carlyle gig on short notice and had to fly right back from Florida."

"Lies one and two," Stone said. "Try harder."

"What do you mean 'lies one and two'?"

"One: you made the Carlyle booking eight weeks ago. Two: you didn't go to Florida. I'm still listening."

"All right, here's some truth: watch your back."

"I guess that's always good advice. Should I watch for anything or anyone in particular?"

"If Sal wants you dead, you'll never see it coming."

"I don't know anyone named Sal."

"Now who's lying? I was sitting with him last night at the restaurant!"

"I didn't know anyone at that table except you, and I'm not so sure about you."

"Sal Trafficante is the number two man in the East Coast mob," she said. "His dining companion was Antonio Datilla, who's number one."

"You know such interesting people," Stone said. "Why would this Sal be concerned with my back?"

"Because of me."

"Have I been unknowingly competing with Sal for your affections?"

"Sal thinks so, except for the 'unknowingly' part."

"Is Sal a psychic in his spare time?"

"Pretty much," she replied.

"Well, let's do a little ESP," Stone said. "I'd never seen nor heard of Sal until last night. The only person I know who is acquainted with Sal is you. Ergo, you told Sal that I was his competition."

"Not exactly. He figured it out."

"Based on what knowledge?"

"I may have said something that included your name."

"What sort of something?"

"Something in bed."

"What did you tell Sal about me?"

"Nothing. He had never heard your name until I spoke it."

"In bed?"

"Yes."

"What did you say, exactly, about me?"

"Nothing."

"But you spoke my name?"

"I screamed your name!!! When Sal and I were fucking!!! Now do you get it?"

Stone was momentarily at a loss for words. "I hope you lied to him," he said, finally.

"What could I say? That I made up somebody else's name while I was fucking him?"

"That would have been a start."

"I said it was the name of an old boyfriend from college," she said. "That didn't work."

"What worked?"

"The truth. It was all I had left."

"And that worked?"

"Well, he didn't beat me up, so I guess so."

"Did you tell him who I was?"

"I didn't need to. It took him about three minutes to have somebody, ah, research you. It's not a common name, you know."

"What else does he know about me?"

"Have you ever googled yourself?"

"Not for a long time."

"Maybe you'd better have a look at Wikipedia."

"Maybe I'd better," Stone admitted.

"Look, this will blow over. I can convince him that you're nothing to me."

"How long will that take?"

"I don't know. I won't be bringing up your name, though."

"That's good to know, but not very comforting."

"I could come over there and comfort you," she said.

"I think that would be an apocalyptic lapse in judgment," Stone said.

"He won't know. He's already left town."

"I expect he's acquainted with persons who have not left town. And from what you've told me, they could be following you, as well as me."

"You think so?"

"What phone are you talking on?" Stone asked.

"The phone in my suite, at the Carlyle."

"Oh, swell," Stone said. "That's really confidential. He's probably already hired a staff member to give him a daily rundown on your calls in his absence."

"I didn't think of that. Next time I'll use a throwaway."

"Listen to me, Hilda. You cannot communicate with me by any means."

"For how long?"

"Forever is almost long enough. If he learns something that will make him want to kill me, he will probably include you on his revenge list."

"All right, I won't call again."

"Or write or e-mail or FedEx or send carrier pigeons."

"Oh, all right."

"Then goodbye, my dear. I hope we'll both live long enough to meet again after somebody has put two in Mr. Trafficante's head." He hung up.

He had only one thought. **Jesus, what a mess!**

34

Stone made it to Patroon by eight-thirty. As he entered, he looked to his usual table and saw Dino drinking with a woman whose back was to him, but who was not Viv. It didn't look like Hilda, either.

He approached the table cautiously. It was Tara Wilkes. She stood up and hugged him. "I'm so sorry for my behavior last night," she said.

He held her a little away from him and looked into her eyes. "Why are you sorry?"

"I had an unreasonable fit of jealousy, and I behaved badly. Will you forgive me?"

"Nothing to forgive," Stone said, reseating her, then seating himself.

"Welcome back into the fold," Dino said.

"Who?"

"You."

"Please excuse me," Tara said, and allowed herself to be steered toward the ladies'.

"Me back in the fold? I thought it was Tara, and the fold was mine."

"It's a female thing," Dino said. "She asks your forgiveness, but what she's really doing is forgiving you."

"You've been reading **Cosmopolitan**, haven't you?"

"Sometimes I pick it up at the barbershop," Dino admitted. "It's unisex. You look like you don't feel well," he said.

"I don't particularly. I mean, I'm not sick, I've just had some bad news."

"Share with me. Maybe that will help."

He told Dino about his conversation with Hilda Ross.

Dino's eyes widened. "She screamed your name while in Trafficante's arms? That's unbelievable!"

"Trafficante believed it. It didn't take him long to get a fix on me, either. He knows everything but my underwear size and Social Security number."

"Is Sal the jealous type?"

"Yes, and one who can turn jealousy into revenge in a flash."

"So that's why he looked at you that way last night?"

"Here comes Tara," Stone said. "Try to look cheerful and unconcerned."

"Sure," Dino said, pasting a wide smile on his face. Stone did the same.

Tara sat down. "What are you two so happy about?"

"Just happy to see you," Stone said, working on keeping the smile in place.

"How nice," she said doubtfully.

"Really," Stone said. "Really glad to see you."

"Stone was telling me he's going to take a vacation," Dino said.

Stone glared at him. "Is that your advice, Dino?"

"In the circumstances, why not?"

"What circumstances?" Tara asked.

"Stone is feeling a little crowded in New York."

"Dino," Stone said. "Please stop talking."

Dino raised his hands in surrender.

"Where are you thinking of going, Stone?"

"Do you think you could take a week off from your work?" Stone asked. "Maybe two?"

"Well, my preseason shows ended today, and my supervisors have got the new patterns in hand, so there's not really much for me to do for a while but complain. And I'm sure my people could do without that."

"I'll pick you up at eight tomorrow morning," Stone said. "Bring your passport, casual outdoor clothes, a sweater, some walking shoes, and a dress or three for the evenings."

"How serious are the evenings?"

"From casual to black tie. You never know."

"And I'm not supposed to ask where we're going?"

"Right."

"How about Viv and me?" Dino asked. "Can we come?"

"Sure, glad to have you."

"Stone," Tara said, "you mentioned you have an airplane. Is it big enough for four people and their luggage?"

"Yes," Stone replied. "And a dog. I'm inviting Bob."

"How many bags may I bring?" Tara asked.

"About one camel load."

"Better make it two camel loads," Dino said. "Viv will bring that much."

"There's room for that?" Tara asked.

"Don't worry about it," Dino said.

"Are we flying east or west?"

"Don't ask," Stone said.

"When will I know?"

"When we get there. You can bring a compass, if you'd like an early warning."

A waiter brought a menu.

"Osso bucco," Stone said.

"Me, too," Tara echoed.

"Chicken paillard," Dino said.

"And a bottle of the Pine Ridge cabernet," Stone said, handing back the meus. The waiter fled.

"Do you ride?" Stone asked.

"Yes," Tara said. "Shall I bring a saddle?"

"Just your habit and boots. I think we can find you a helmet."

"How about a crop?"

"All right, but to be used only on the horse."

"Will I have time to read?"

"Yes, but we have books at our disposal, if you don't want to carry a book bag."

"Anything else?"

"A raincoat. We can supply you with gum boots and an umbrella, should you need them."

"So it rains where we're going."

"It rains almost everywhere," Stone said. "We are not visiting a desert region. And stop trying to figure out where we're going. It's more fun this way."

"Sounds like Ireland."

"Maybe, maybe not." Stone held up a hand. "I shall have no further comment on geography," he said.

Dinner came, and Tara asked no further questions.

At one point, when she opened her mouth to ask something, Stone raised a finger. "Ah, ah."

"Oh, all right, I'll shut up," she said, pouting.

"You don't have to shut up; just don't ask travel questions. You already know more than you need to know."

"Well, this is going to be interesting," Tara said.

"Let's hope it doesn't get too interesting," Dino replied.

35

Stone called his pilot, Faith. "Wheels up tomorrow at nine AM, for Windward Hall. We'll need a copilot and a stewardess."

"Consider it done," Faith said, then hung up.

"Windward Hall? Is that where we're going?" Tara asked.

Stone put a finger to his lips, and she retreated.

"Sounds like the Bahamas to me," Tara said to Dino.

Dino put a finger to his lips.

"When are you going to tell Viv about this?" she asked Dino.

"I already have," he said, hitting send on a text.

Tara's shoulders sagged. "I give up," she said.

"Good," Stone said. "You'll enjoy the experience more that way."

"Have you told Bob?"

"I'll explain it to him when I get home."

* * *

Stone picked up Tara at the appointed hour the following morning, and a half hour later, they were at Teterboro. Fred pulled the car into the Strategic Services hangar alongside the airplane, a Gulfstream 500, and linemen unloaded and stowed the luggage.

"I don't suppose I'll be able to get to my bags if I've forgotten a hairbrush or something," Tara said.

"Of course you will," Stone replied. "The baggage compartment is accessible from the rear cabin." He escorted her aboard the airplane, showed her the layout, seated her, and turned her over to the stewardess, while he went forward. "Excuse me," he said to Tara, "I have to go fly the airplane."

"You didn't tell me about that part," Tara called after him.

"Stone likes to take off and land the airplane. Keeps his pilot's skills sharp," the stewardess said. She left Tara with coffee and pastries, then went to deal with Dino and Viv.

From the right seat, Faith read off the preflight checklist, while Stone set the switches and repeated the commands to her. He called the tower for permission to taxi and received clearance to runway one. He ran through the final checklist, then requested takeoff.

"Cleared for takeoff," the woman in the tower said. Stone steered the aircraft onto the runway, using the tiller, then pushed the throttles all the way forward. The airplane began to roll. A moment later, he had enough airspeed for steerage with the rudder and used his feet to keep them on the center line, while Faith called out his speeds, "Seventy knots, one hundred knots," then, "Rotate!"

Stone pulled steadily back on the yoke, and the airplane lifted off. A moment later he retracted the landing gear and flaps, then he switched on the autopilot, and that instrument flew the airplane through the departure procedure, turning northeast, along the north shore of Long Island. At that point, Stone gave the airplane back to Faith, her copilot joined her, and he returned to his seat with his guests.

"Okay, we're off!" Tara said. "Now can I know where we're going?"

"You won't know until we arrive," Stone said.

Tara looked out the window and saw the eastern tip of Long Island pass. "We're out over the ocean!" she said.

"Right where we're supposed to be," Stone replied. "This might be a good time to brief you on the location of your life jacket and our life raft."

"Why do we need those?" she asked.

"Just in case we get our feet wet."

Tara pretended to faint.

Bob, who had boarded last, came to greet everybody.

"See, Bob's not worried," Stone said.

"He's a dog," Tara pointed out.

"And a very smart one," Stone replied.

Bob settled into his travel bed across the aisle, and in a minute was sound asleep. "See?" Stone said. "Nothing to worry about."

"How long is our flight?" Tara asked.

"We'll have lunch aboard and we'll be on the ground in time for dinner."

"Sounds like Ireland," she said, consulting a small compass she had brought along.

"Does it?" Stone picked up the **Times**, found the crossword and gave the rest to Tara. "Here," he said, "improve your mind. There's a piece about Ireland in the business section."

Tara flipped through the paper until she found it. "It's about butter production," she said.

"I'll bet there's a lot you don't know about butter production," Stone replied.

After the **Times**, lunch was served: a lobster salad and a chilled bottle of Far Niente chardonnay. After that, people tended to drift off, Tara with her head on Stone's shoulder.

* * *

Eventually, lights appeared along the southwest coast of England. Shortly after that, the airplane gave a jerk, waking Tara.

"What was that?"

"The landing gear coming down."

"Is it supposed to do that?"

"It's mandatory before landing. Do this." He pinched his nose and blew, clearing his ears.

"Who's landing the airplane?"

"That tiny blonde you saw when we boarded."

"Where are we?"

"Approaching the runway at Windward Hall."

"What's Windward Hall?"

"A very nice house."

"Where is it?"

"Dead ahead." They touched down, rolled out, and stopped. The engines died, and the stewardess opened the cabin door. A Range Rover and a golf cart with a truck bed awaited them at the bottom of the airstairs.

They got into the Range Rover, and Bob hopped on the golf cart, next to the driver. The caravan moved off, toward the well-lighted main house in the distance.

"Is that a movie set?" Tara asked, pointing at the house.

"No, it is a country house in the county of Hampshire, in the south of England."

"Whose is it?"

"Mine."

"Oh. I guess we're there then."

"We are there. Are you disappointed?"

"To the contrary, I'm very impressed. And hungry."

"Dinner will be served as soon as you've unpacked and freshened up."

"You don't seem to have any luggage, except your briefcase."

"I have a wardrobe here. It's not necessary to bring things from New York." He led her upstairs to the master suite, and showed her to her dressing room and bath. "I'll see you in the library as soon as you're done," he said. "Bottom of the stairs, then right."

Ten minutes later she joined the others as Stone was tending bar. "Scotch?" he asked.

"Laphroaig, if you have it."

"We have." He poured the drink and handed it to her. She took a seat and looked around the paneled room, stocked with leather-bound volumes. "Have you read all these books?" she asked.

"Not yet."

They sat down before the fire and sipped.

"Now that the mystery of our destination is solved, here's another: Why are we here?"

"To keep Stone from being murdered in the street," Dino replied. He raised his glass. "I give you Stone, not dead."

They all drank.

36

They had a tomato and basil bisque, followed by a pork roast, with vegetables from the garden, followed by an apple tart, then Stilton and port.

"All right," Tara said. "I've contained my curiosity long beyond the ability of most adults: Why is someone trying to murder you, Stone?"

"Jealous lover," he said.

"A woman?"

"Male jealous lover."

"Who is the woman involved?"

"Caravaggio, the night before last. Now, is your curiosity satisfied?"

"Details, please."

"I've no wish to speak ill of her, and the details would not be complimentary of her judgment, so I will avoid those. Are you curious about nothing else?"

"All right, how did you come to own this house?"

"A friend of mine who lives across the Beaulieu River"—he pronounced it **Bewley**—"found me on the continent and insisted I come and see it. She didn't tell me at the time that 'it' was an estate, just said it would be a nice surprise. It was."

"Then?"

"She gave me the tour. Then she introduced me to the owner, who had been ill and was not getting better, over dinner at the Royal Yacht Squadron, in Cowes, across the Solent. There, I wrote him a check for the property."

"What is the 'Solent'?"

"The body of water that separates mainland England from the Isle of Wight."

"Who was this friend?"

"Her name is Dame Felicity Devonshire. You will meet her at dinner here tomorrow evening."

"What is the 'Royal Yacht Squadron'?"

"It is the oldest yacht club in England, second oldest in the world after the Royal Cork Yacht Club in Ireland. It is housed in a seaside castle built by Henry the Eighth, to protect England from the French."

"Will we dine there while we're in England?"

"If I survive long enough."

They moved to the sofa and chairs before

the fireplace for brandy. Stone's phone rang. He looked at the caller ID and saw the word **Private**. "Excuse me," he said, "I have to take this." He walked into the hallway and pressed the button. "Hello?"

"Stone?"

"Who is this?"

"It's Hilda."

"Sorry, I didn't recognize your voice."

"I'm calling from a rather small powder room."

"I won't inquire further about that."

"I have good news: you're off the hook."

"How so?"

"Sal has left town."

"Good. When is he coming back?"

"It sounded as though he had quite a lot to do elsewhere."

"Where did he go?"

"Out of the country. That's why you don't have to worry."

"Where is he as we speak?"

"In London."

Swell, Stone thought. "Why London?"

"He said he had business to take care of there."

"Thanks for letting me know. I have guests, so I have to go now."

"Sure. I just wanted you to be able to relax."

"I'm grateful to you, Hilda. Bye-bye."

He returned to the library.

Dino's eyebrows went up. "You don't look so hot," he said. "What's wrong?"

"I've just learned that I have nothing to worry about," Stone said. "Sal has left New York."

"That's good news."

"The bad news is, he's gone to London."

Everybody was silent for a moment.

"How far is London?" Tara asked, finally.

"About eighty miles—an hour-and-a-half drive."

"Oh. Does he know you are . . . wherever we are?"

"The nearest village is Beaulieu. I have no reason to believe he knows I'm here."

"Well, then, he might as well be anywhere," Tara said. "So might you be."

"I prefer three thousand miles from him to eighty," Stone said, "given the choice."

"It's rather ironic that we've come all the way here to get away from this man, and he turns out to be eighty miles away."

"I got the irony, thanks," Stone said.

"What will you do?"

"Stay put, and not tell anybody where I am. That's what you should do, too."

"I haven't told anybody," Tara said. "Except my production manager, Tony. He has to be able to get in touch with me, if there are production problems."

Dino took a notebook and pen from his pocket. "I'll make a list," he said. "What's Tony's last name?"

"Trafficante," Tara replied, spelling it for him.

"I know how to spell it," Dino said, looking at Stone. "You know, sometimes I think you're the luckiest guy in the world, but then sometimes . . . not so much."

"When did you speak to him?" Stone asked.

"Right after we arrived. I didn't know where we were going until then, remember?"

"Did you swear him to secrecy?"

"I didn't know our whereabouts were a secret, except from me."

"Tell me about Tony Trafficante," Dino said. "Where's he from?"

"Born and raised in Brooklyn."

"Do you know if he has any relatives in . . . unusual occupations?"

"What sort of unusual occupations?"

"Bookmaking, loan-sharking, prostitution, like that."

"You mean, like, criminal occupations?"

"I do."

"Well, there were rumors about his family when we were kids."

"What sort of rumors?"

"Like, **unusual** occupations."

"Tara," Stone said. "What, exactly, did you tell Tony about where we were?"

"I told him I was in a beautiful country house named Windward Hall, in the county of Hampshire, in the south of England. In short, exactly what you told me."

"Oh," Stone said.

37

Everyone was very quiet, even Tara, until she finally got it.

"Oh," she said.

"Think hard, Tara," Stone said. "Has Tony ever mentioned anyone in his family called Sal?"

"No, I don't think so." She thought some more. "Does 'Salvatore' count?"

"Oh, yeah," Dino said, making another note in his notebook.

"It counts," Stone said. "How are they related?"

Tara thought about it. "I don't know. The name was mentioned only once in my hearing."

"In what context?"

"That Salvatore was a real piece of shit," she said. "That was about it."

"Well, I'm glad they aren't chummy," Stone said.

"I didn't say they weren't chummy," Tara replied. "My recollection is that they are **very** chummy. That's why Tony can talk about him that way."

"Does Tony spend a lot of time in Brooklyn?"

"He lives there, with his mother."

"Does his mother have any siblings?"

"A sister. Just one."

"Does the sister have any children?"

"Just one. Tony is an only child, too."

"Is Tony's aunt's son Salvatore?"

"Yes, that's it."

"Tara," Stone said, "I want you to call Tony. It's late afternoon in New York, so he shouldn't be hard to find."

"No, he should be at work," she said. "What am I to say to him?"

"I want to know if he's told anyone else about where we are, using the references that you heard from me. I want to know if Sal knows, and if Tony knows why Sal went to London. Put the call on speaker, so we can all hear."

"Why shall I say I'm calling?"

"Just checking in, everything all right? Like that. Then, casually, ask him if he's told anyone where you are."

"All right." She dug her phone from her purse, dialed a number, pressed the speaker button, and set the phone on the coffee table.

"Tony speaking."

"Hi, Tony, it's Tara. How are you?"

"I thought you were on vacation in Paris."

Tara started to correct him, but Stone waved both arms. "That's right, I am. I just wanted to see if the new production is moving along."

"It's right where it's supposed to be at this point," Tony said, sounding exasperated.

"Tony: question for you."

"Okay."

"Remember, earlier today, when I called and told you where I am?"

"Yeah, I remember."

"Have you mentioned that to anybody?"

"Yeah, I mentioned it to Mama. We talk a couple of times a day, and she likes to know what's going on."

"And you told her I was in Paris?"

"Yeah, I . . . Wait a minute, did I say Paris?"

"You tell me."

"It was south of something. Did I say Paris?"

"Yes, you did."

"Then that must be what I told her."

"Do you think she might have told somebody else what you said?"

"She doesn't talk to anybody but me— Oh, and her sister."

"Is that the sister who is the mother of Salvatore?"

"Yeah, Sal. That piece of shit."

Stone put his face in his hands and groaned.

"Why don't you like Sal, Tony?"

"Well, I don't **dislike** him. He's just a piece of shit."

"Is that what you call somebody you like?"

"Well, I don't like him **that** much."

"He clearly rubs you the wrong way."

"He always has, since we were kids."

"Do you speak to him often?"

"Not if I can help it."

"Are you likely to speak to him anytime soon?"

"Sometimes he brings his mother over to see my mother, and they have tea. That's about the only time."

"How often?"

"Usually on Friday."

Stone winced.

"So they could be there today?"

"Probably."

"Tony, I'd appreciate it if you'd do me a favor."

"Sure, what's that?"

"If you should see Sal or his mother, please don't mention what I said to you about being where I am."

"Why not?"

"Because Sal dislikes a man I know. He may even want to hurt him."

"Well, I wouldn't want to be the guy Sal wants to hurt. He's sort of in the hurt business, if you know what I mean."

Stone shook his head and mouthed, **Don't ask.**

"What do you mean?"

"Well, if you want somebody's legs broken or a throat cut, Sal always knows somebody who knows somebody, you know?"

"I do now. Please remember what I said about Sal, Tony."

"Oh, I forgot. Sal won't be here today. He went to London."

Stone made beckoning motions and mouthed, **Why?**

"Why did Sal go to London?"

"He said he had to see a man about a dog."

"Okay."

"No, that's wrong. He said he had a throat to cut."

Stone gritted his teeth. He mouthed, **Hang up.**

"Do you know where he stays in London?"

"Yeah, in that hotel where Elizabeth Taylor and Eddie Fisher used to stay. The big one."

"Gotta run, Tony. Take care." Tara hung up.

"Where did Elizabeth Taylor and Eddie Fisher used to stay?" Stone asked.

Dino began typing on his iPhone with his thumbs. "The Dorchester," he said. "They stayed there while she was making **Cleopatra** and screwing Richard Burton at the same time."

"Is that what it says on Wikipedia?" Stone asked.

"It's what they wanted to say," Dino replied.

"How did I do?" Tara asked.

"Nice, how you ran with the Paris thing," Dino said.

"Stone?"

"Yeah, the part about Paris worked. I hope."

38

Finally, everyone went upstairs. Bob curled up in his bed beside the fireplace.

Tara seemed to like the master suite. "I like the master suite," she said.

"I'm glad. It likes you, too."

She came out of her dressing room wearing a black sheath nightgown.

"It likes you better without the nightgown," he said.

She stopped at the bedside, shucked off the shoulder straps, and let it fall to the floor. "Like this?"

"Like that," Stone said, pulling her to him and kissing her on the belly, then working his way down.

"Mmmm, I'm glad you like that," Tara said, doing what she could to help him. "Tell me about Dame Felicity Devonshire," she said.

Stone stopped what he was doing. "Now?"

"Oh, okay, let's finish, then you can tell me about her."

He finished, and she expressed approval and appropriate gratitude.

"You're welcome," he said.

"Now Dame Felicity. How old is she? Let's start with that."

"No one knows," Stone said.

"I bet I could find out."

"You might want to steer away from that inquiry. It's probably covered by the Official Secrets Act."

"And what is that?"

"It's a document that about half the British population has signed, swearing not to reveal any Official Secrets. Violating it could get you sent to prison."

"Do you know how old she is?"

"Probably, but for reasons just stated I cannot discuss the subject."

"Is she younger or older than I? Is that an 'Official Secret'?"

"Maybe not, but I can only guess."

"Which?"

"It's probably best to say that she is of an indeterminate age."

"Ah. Older, then."

"You said that, not I."

"Is she beautiful?"

"Oh, yes. Nothing indeterminate about that."

"Does she like men?"

"Certainly."

"Does she like women?"

"Now, there we're straying into Official Secrets territory again."

"So she likes women, as well as men?"

"Why do you want to know? Are you aiming at seducing her?"

"I don't know, yet. Would she object, if I did?"

"Probably not."

"Would you object if I seduced her?"

"Not if I can watch."

Tara laughed. "Wouldn't you rather help?"

"It's my nature to be helpful," Stone replied.

"Does she work?"

"Oh, yes, ah . . . Do you mean does she have a job?"

"I do."

"She works for the British government, in the Foreign Office."

"What's the Foreign Office?"

"It's like our State Department. It conducts foreign affairs."

"What does she do in the Foreign Office?"

"She holds an executive position."

"Why are you trying so hard not to tell me what she does? Is it an Official Secret?"

"It used to be, until a newspaper printed the name of one of her predecessors. After that, there hardly seemed to be a point."

"Then, if I can read it in a newspaper, you shouldn't mind telling me."

"All right, if we were living in a James Bond novel, she would be called 'M.' She is the director of MI-6, which is the foreign intelligence service."

"Like our CIA?"

"Yes."

"Is there an MI something else?"

"There's MI-5, which is the domestic intelligence service, sort of like our FBI. "I don't know if there are other MIs."

"Dame Felicity sounds more and more interesting," Tara said.

"She is certainly 'more and more interesting,'" Stone agreed.

"She sounds very smart."

"She is that, and a specialty of hers is upending persons who fail to perceive that."

"I like smart, beautiful women," Tara said.

"That makes two of us."

She stretched out beside him and fondled his nether region. "I believe, as the saying goes, I owe you one."

"You're halfway there," Stone said, making himself available.

* * *

When Stone awoke the curtains had been pulled back, and sunlight was streaming through the windows. Tara was still naked and laying out her riding habit on her side of the bed.

"Good morning," she said.

"And to you. I take it you would like to go riding this morning."

"I would."

"May I persuade you to have some breakfast first?"

"You may. I'd like what is called on hotel menus, a 'full English breakfast.'"

"With or without a kipper?"

"You want to have sex during breakfast?" she asked.

"A kipper is a smoked herring."

"With **breakfast**?"

"It's very popular with breakfast."

"All right, I'll give it a try."

Stone called down and ordered.

Breakfast arrived. Tara tasted her kipper and was pleased.

"I'm glad."

"I saw something last night."

"Asleep or awake?"

"I think awake, but I can't be sure."

"What did you see?"

"I got out of bed and pulled back that curtain," she said, pointing at a window.

"What did you see?"

"The lawn was moonlit, and I saw a figure run across it."

"A figure? A figure of what?"

"A figure of a man. At least, I think it was a man. It was dressed in black, from head to toe."

"And where did it run from and to?"

"From there," she said, pointing in the direction of the Beaulieu River, "to there." She pointed toward the front gate.

"Was he carrying anything?"

"Such as?"

"Such as a weapon. A rifle, perhaps."

"I can't be sure, since I'm not sure I was awake."

"Well, as we ride, we'll look for evidence of an intruder."

"Good idea," she said.

They both got into their riding clothes, and Stone pulled on a shoulder holster, shoved a small 9mm pistol into it, then slipped into a tweed jacket. "Ready?"

"Oh, yes."

39

The horses awaited them in the stable yard, held by a girl groom. Another groom gave them each a leg up, Stone onto his favorite gelding and Tara onto a pretty mare. Someone handed her a helmet, and she tried it on. "Good."

"Don't forget to buckle the strap," Stone said, buckling his own.

"What are the horses' names?" Tara asked.

"I don't think we've ever been properly introduced," Stone replied.

The girl groom spoke up. "The gelding is Casey, the mare Connie. And my name is Peg. Your lunch is tied onto Casey's saddle."

"Thank you, Peg," Stone said, and headed for the long front lawn, leading down to the airstrip and its hangar. Tara pulled up even with him, and they walked their mounts to warm them up.

"Keep an eye out for the ninja," Stone said.

"That's what he looked like, a ninja."

"Do you often wake in the middle of the night and see things you aren't sure are there?"

"Not as a regular thing," Tara replied, "but it has been known to happen."

"Did any of these sightings turn out to be real?"

"Not exactly. They just seemed real to me."

"Then I won't shoot first and ask questions later. We wouldn't want to wing a girl groom."

"Why do you call them 'girl grooms'?" she asked. "It seems demeaning."

"Because they're young girls and they are grooms. It's a traditional title around stables. If you like, you can take them aside and question them about their feelings on that subject. If it seems indicated, we'll rename them."

"Rename them what?"

"That can be between you and the grooms."

"Fair enough."

"Let's gallop a bit. Are you comfortable with jumping?"

"Why?"

"Because there's a stone wall a couple of hundred yards ahead that requires either jumping or getting down and opening a gate, then closing it behind us, so the cattle won't get out."

"I'll jump," she said.

"Then lead the way."

She tapped the mare's flanks with her heels and

pulled ahead, while Stone followed, ready
if she didn't make the jump.

Tara took the wall successfully and Stone followed. As the gelding cleared the wall, Stone glimpsed something out of the corner of his eye. A man, he thought, and dressed in black. By the time he could rein up and call out to Tara, the shape had vanished into the brush.

"What?" she asked.

"I think I saw your figure in black," Stone said, turning his horse toward the bushes. He got down from his mount, unbuttoned his jacket for access to his firearm, then he tied Casey to a branch. "Wait here," he called to Tara.

"All right."

He parted the bushes and made his way toward the main road, unable to see more than a few yards ahead. He unholstered the pistol, racked the slide, and flipped on the safety. Up ahead he could see a small roof rising above the brush. It was called the Hermit's Cottage, where an actual hermit had once lived. He made his way there and peeked through a window. The two rooms were bare.

He circumnavigated the cottage, then walked back to where the horses were. "Nothing," he said. "Nothing I could see, anyway. We need to clear these woods of the undergrowth." He got a foot into a stirrup and swung aboard the gelding, then they walked on toward the airstrip.

"Why is there an airfield here?" Tara asked.

"During the war, the big one, World War II, there was a training camp on the property for intelligence agents who would be parachuted into France. The airstrip was built so they would have one that wasn't on the charts, and they camouflaged it. They even had a couple of buildings that could be rolled on and off the runway, to make it look like a farm from the air. After the war, when the property was restored to its owners, they kept up the strip, and the last owner before me repaved it as part of an estate-wide renovation of the property. It's seven thousand feet long and accommodates my Gulfstream very nicely. After we land, a fuel truck is sent over from Southampton Airport to top us off. They sometimes, but not always, send a customs team over to gaze at our passports. It's very convenient."

"Judging from what I've seen of your life, you're very good at making things convenient," Tara said.

"It's part of my native sloth," Stone explained, "to have things set up that way."

They walked over to the hangar, and Stone dismounted, handed Tara his reins, and walked over to the door. He examined the padlock and found some scratches on it and scarring on the hangar door around the hasp. "Looks like someone has tried to gain entry," he said.

He took a clump of keys from his pocket, unlocked it, and pressed a remote control on his key ring. The door slid upward and back, revealing the Gulfstream. Stone did a slow walk-around, looking for anything amiss, but found nothing.

"Are you getting paranoid?" Tara asked when he returned.

"Maybe just a little," he said. He led the horses beyond the hangar to a tree, where he tied them and helped Tara down, then he got their lunch from his saddle.

They were munching away at smoked salmon sandwiches and drinking a nice hock when Tara's phone rang. She looked at the caller ID, then got to her feet. "Excuse me, business call." She walked a few yards away and had a few minutes' conversation, then hung up and came back.

"That was Tony," she said. "We've burnt up the motor on one of our machines, and he's had to shut down production until we can replace it."

"Any news of his cousin, Salvatore?"

"I asked, and he reminded me that his cousin is out of the country."

"I was hoping he had come home," Stone said.

"Oh, well, we're not in London, are we?"

"I think I'll look into his exact whereabouts at first opportunity," Stone said.

"How will you do that?"

"I have a friend who has people who are good at that sort of thing."

"That sounds like the fabled Dame Felicity."

"Could be."

"I can't wait to meet her."

40

Stone practiced his Cary Grant trick of tying his bow tie in a single, smooth motion, then got into his waistcoat, buttoned it, and settled his pocket watch and its gold chain into the pockets, then he got into the naval-length jacket.

Tara was passing his dressing room and stopped. “What sort of uniform are you wearing?” she asked.

“It’s the dress uniform of the Royal Yacht Squadron, which is worn in nautical situations. I’m wearing it tonight because our guest, and Felicity’s date, is the new commodore of the Squadron, Sir Thomas Callaway, whose wife is otherwise occupied this evening.”

“And is this a nautical situation?”

“The Beaulieu River is right over there and there are lots of boats moored upon it.”

"Are you going to invite Dame Felicity up here after dinner?"

"I thought I would leave our after-dinner disposition to you and Dame Felicity, once you've each had an opportunity to inspect the other and get to know one another. I will abide by the wishes of the two of you, whatever they may be."

"So, you're remaining neutral in the matter?"

"I'm remaining flexible. Do with me as you will."

"What more could a girl—or two girls—ask?"

"I'm sure you'll both think of something."

She turned her back to be zipped, and Stone obliged.

"You're very good at that," Tara said.

"I'm better at the unzipping," Stone replied.

"You will have that opportunity."

They walked down the stairs and turned into the library, where Dino and Viv awaited, drinks already in hand. A young man poured Stone's and Tara's.

"What is that young man called in the household?" Tara asked.

"In the old days, he would have been called a footman, but nowadays we call him a bartender—or a stable hand, which is his day job.

"How was your day?" Stone asked the Bacchettis.

"Spent in bed, reading," Viv said. "Mostly reading, anyway. She batted her eyes at Dino.

"We went riding this morning and had a picnic lunch," Stone said.

The door opened, and Geoffrey, the butler, called out, "Sir Thomas Callaway and Dame Felicity Devonshire."

Stone introduced everyone who had not already been introduced. Felicity leaned close to kiss Stone on the cheek, and she whispered, "She's scrumptious." Stone winked at Tara, who blushed.

Callaway shook Tara's hand. "It's Tommy, if you please."

"I please," Tara replied, and the two of them began an animated conversation with the Bacchettis.

Stone momentarily had Felicity to himself, and he used the opportunity.

"I wonder if I might impose on your good nature?" he asked her.

"Do you wish someone shot?" she asked, archly.

"Well, that is devoutly to be wished, but too soon to act upon. I'd like to find someone in London."

"Someone of some consequence, I take it."

"Yes, an American Mafioso named Salvatore Trafficante. There is a rumor, unconfirmed, that he is staying at the Dorchester. If I know where to find him, I can have him watched."

"Do you employ a watcher, or do you wish me to provide that service, as well?"

"I would not so impose upon you, but a location would make my life easier—and safer."

"Stone, don't tell me someone is after your scalp—not again."

"I'm afraid so."

"And what, pray, are the circumstances?"

"Boring. A jealous lover."

"I am shocked, but not surprised."

"I don't even know the fellow. We saw her on different occasions, and he assigned more importance to our relationship than was justified. Alas, he employs people who make people go away, and I am very happy, here on planet Earth."

"Consider it done. And I may, in turn, ask a favor of you, before our evening is over." Her eyes traveled toward Tara.

"I will leave that matter in your capable hands, and hers," Stone said. "But I am here to assist in any way I'm asked."

"You are a dear," Felicity said, "and I'm sure, so is she."

"You are an excellent judge of character," Stone said.

"And of flesh," Felicity replied. Then they were joined by others and she stepped aside. "Excuse me, phone call." She walked to a corner of the room and spoke for a moment, then came back.

"Nothing that would require you to leave us, I hope," Stone said.

"Oh, no, nothing like that. I would not allow myself to be torn away from this happy scene."

In due course, they were called to dinner in the small dining room.

"I've seen your Hinckley in the Squadron marina," Tommy Callaway said to Stone. "Very handsome."

"Yes, I've abandoned the adventure of sail for the comforts of motorboating," Stone replied.

"Oh?"

"Yes. Also, I was unable to find a woman willing to be both cook and foredeck gorilla."

"It is a rare one who is highly qualified for both," the commodore agreed.

"Also, for some reason, they don't like being shouted at," Stone said, "which is a big part of working the foredeck."

"That way lies disaster," Tommy agreed.

Stone looked down the table and took note of the animated conversation between Tara and Felicity, both of them talking right past Dino, who was trying not to look bored.

After dinner, they adjourned to the library for brandy. Bob left his place by the fire and graciously greeted each of the guests, presenting himself for a petting or a back scratch. He finally settled under Felicity's hand, as if the proper place for it was on his head.

Somehow they had gathered before the fire with the ladies at one end and the gentlemen at the other.

"You looked bored during dinner," Stone said to Dino.

"With the conversation, yes," Dino replied, "but the cleavage was electrifying."

41

The Bacchettis excused themselves and went upstairs to bed. Shortly after that, Tommy Callaway left, too, explaining that he and Felicity had arrived in their own boats. This left Stone alone with Tara and Felicity.

"Shall we?" Tara said to Felicity.

"Oh, yes," Felicity replied. "And, Stone, you can come, too."

Stone's cell phone chose that moment to ring. A check of the caller ID revealed it to be the managing partner of Woodman & Weld. "I have to take this call," he said to the women. "I'll join you as soon as I can get rid of him."

The women seemed happy to start without him.

"Hello, Bill," Stone said.

"What time is it there? Am I calling too late?"

"It's eleven o'clock. What is it?"

"I've got Steele on a conference call, so I'm switching you in."

He did so, before Stone could stop him.

"Stone?"

"Arthur," he replied. Arthur Steele's insurance companies were Stone's largest and most boring account. He settled in for nearly an hour of hemming and hawing, then was finally released.

Weary, but looking forward to what was to come, Stone trudged up the stairs and turned the knob on the door of the master suite. It was locked. Never mind, he thought, I have a master key. He did, but it was not in his pocket; he realized he must have left it on his dresser. He rapped lightly on the door, waited, then rapped as hard as he felt he could without disturbing the Bacchettis. He put an ear to the thick, oaken door: nothing.

He tried, first, Tara's cell phone, then Felicity's. Both went straight to voicemail. "Unlock the door," he responded to both of them.

He rested his forehead against the door and resisted the temptation to fall asleep standing up. Finally, with no other recourse, he wandered down the hallway and entered the nearest vacant guest room. He shed his Squadron mess kit, crawled into the bed, and was asleep almost instantly.

* * *

He awoke in a sunlit room, an hour later than he usually did, and found himself alone. He thought about it, then gathered his clothing and marched down the hall to the master suite and hammered on the door, not caring whom he woke.

After a minute or so, the door was opened by a sleepy Tara, who was naked. "What are you doing out there?" she asked. "We waited for you as long as we could."

Stone walked into the room. "You locked me out," Stone said.

"But you have a master key. You told me."

"You're right. I left it in my dressing room, I'm afraid."

"Oh, baby," she said, kissing him. "And we had such a good time. We both wished you were here. I don't know how to order breakfast. Will you do it, please? I'd like another kipper with my eggs."

Stone called down for breakfast, then got into a shower and a clean nightshirt, so as not to frighten the maid. Breakfast arrived in due course.

"Would you like a blow-by-blow description of last night?"

"Spare me," Stone said.

"Well, suffice it to say, everything went swimmingly. I've never had such fun in bed."

"Thank you. That tops off my morning."

"I mean with another woman. It would have been even better with you here." She squeezed his member. "This would have made all the difference!"

"Thank you, I take that very kindly."

"What happened to you?"

"I got stuck on a meaningless conference call with Bill Eggers and my biggest client, Arthur Steele. I couldn't have made much sense, because all I could think of was you two, upstairs."

"That's sweet," she said, snuggling up to him. "Now, how can I make it up to you?"

Stone was about to tell her when breakfast arrived.

After the breakfast dishes were taken away, Stone made a move toward another foray, but his cell rang. He glanced at it. Felicity.

"Good morning," he said.

"Good morning, my dear. What happened to you last night?"

"I got stuck on a boring conference call for an hour."

"Well, it wasn't boring upstairs," she said, "and we would have enjoyed having you there, so to speak."

"I'm sure I would have enjoyed it, too."

"About your request regarding the resting place of your Mr. Trafficante. He is ensconced in the Oscar Wilde suite at the Savoy and will be there for the remainder of the week. I had two men with nothing to do, so I've posted them there. They will follow him wherever he goes and report directly to you."

"I'm sorry to have put you to that trouble, Felicity."

"No trouble at all, my dear. It keeps them on their toes. Otherwise, they'd probably just nod off in the break room."

Stone thanked her again and hung up. "Salvatore is not at the Dorchester, but at the Savoy, in the Oscar Wilde suite, I daresay their most expensive accommodation."

"Ah."

He set down the phone and made another move on Tara. The phone rang again. Caller ID read: **Private.**

"Yes?"

"Is that Mr. Barrington?"

"It is."

"My name is Jeffers. Dame Felicity directed my partner and me to keep you apprised of the movements of Mr. Trafficante."

"Thank you, she mentioned that."

"Mr. Trafficante, after a five-minute taxi ride, is occupied at his tailor's, in Savile Row."

"Thank you. If you could just note his movements and ring me this afternoon, I'd be grateful."

"Of course, sir. Good day to you."

Stone hung up, rolled over and reached for Tara, but her part of the bed was empty. He heard the shower turn on in her bathroom. He sighed deeply.

Later, in the afternoon, he had another call from Jeffers.

"Sir," he said, "your Mr. Trafficante returned to the Savoy after his tailor's visit and lunch at Cecconi's, and has been ensconced for more than an hour with two young ladies, whom, I suspect, do most of their work in the evenings, if you take my meaning."

"I do, and thank you," Stone said, hanging up. At least **somebody** has a sex life, he reflected.

42

Stone's mood did not improve during the remainder of the day, though he rallied at dinnertime. He, Tara, and the Bacchettis dined in the library and drank a bottle of claret and much of a bottle of port.

At bedtime, he and Tara went freely at each other. As they fell asleep finally, he felt he had made up most of the lost time of the night before. Tara was only one woman, but she was a considerable one, with robust appetites.

The following morning, after sex, breakfast, showering and dressing, he came across a sealed envelope addressed to him. It was from the local constabulary, and postmarked just after his departure from Britain on his last trip over. Inside was a laminated card with his photograph on it and a cover letter from his friend, Chief Constable Holmes.

Dear Stone,

Enclosed please find your long-awaited licence to bear firearms. It is effective in England, Wales, Scotland, Northern Ireland, and all British possessions and members of the Commonwealth for five years.

Kindly recall that it is a licence to carry, not to kill, and you are not, therefore, James Bond. It will, however, prevent your being arrested by any law enforcement official in the aforementioned places for going about armed.

With kind regards

Stone opened his briefcase and got out his passport, which was a diplomatic one, as a consequence of his consulting relationship with the director of Central Intelligence. He reckoned the two IDs, together, would keep him out of jail. He got into a suit and necktie and went downstairs to the library, where everybody was curled up with books.

"What are you all dressed up for?" Tara asked.

"I have to run up to London for a few hours."

She leapt to her feet. "Oh, good, give me a

minute while I get into something for the city." She ran from the room before he could say, "But . . ."

"What are you doing in London?" Dino asked.

"Oh, not much. I'm going to murder Sal Trafficante, if I can get him to stand still long enough."

"Right," Dino said, turning a page. Viv didn't bat an eye.

Tara returned quickly, and Stone went to the safe behind the picture, where there was a stash of cash, and removed a thick stack of sterling currency. "Here's your budget for the day," he said.

A stable hand had brought the Porsche around to the front of the house, and they got in. "Full tank," he said.

"What will you be doing in London?" Tara asked.

"Taking care of business," Stone said, turning onto the road to the village, where he would pick up the motorway.

"Isn't that an Elvis Presley song?" she asked.

"Not today," Stone replied.

They were halfway to London on the motorway when Stone's cell phone rang. "Yes?"

"Mr. Barrington, it's Jeffers here."

"Good morning."

"I thought I would let you know, Mr. Trafficante has not had breakfast yet, and seems to be sleeping in this morning."

"Thank you. Is the Oscar Wilde suite the one facing the river?"

"It is, sir." Jeffers gave him directions from the front desk.

"Is there a suite next door to it?"

"Yes, sir. There is the Gilbert & Sullivan suite abutting it. I'm told that when the occasion requires, the two suites can be made into one, via a door, when unlocked from both sides."

"Is it occupied?"

"I believe not. I saw a bellman take away luggage, and the maid is in there now."

"Please go to the front desk, ask for the manager, and book me into that suite for two nights, using Dame Felicity's name, if necessary. I assume you have been trained in the art of breaking and entering?"

"We call it access of opportunity," Jeffers replied.

"I would like you to practice this art by entering the Oscar Wilde suite and unlocking the adjoining door to the Gilbert & Sullivan suite, without disturbing the occupant. Can you manage that?"

"Of course, sir," Jeffers replied. "It shall be as you wish."

They both hung up.

Tara was staring at him. "Stone . . ."

Stone raised a hand. "Stop," he said. "Don't

ask. You did not hear that conversation and will forget everything you did not hear."

"Where will I be while forgetting this?"

"Shopping. I'll drop you at a convenient spot on the way into town, say Harrods . . ."

"Harvey Nick's," she said.

"Harvey Nick's. And I'll pick you up on the way out of town. When I am headed that way, I will phone you. You will not phone me, got that?"

"Why not?"

"Because I don't want my phone ringing while I'm hiding in a closet or in some other place, but I will not turn it off. You will not text me, either, because my phone makes a noise when receiving a text."

"Gotcha," she said. "Why . . ."

"You do not want to know the why of anything. Anything you buy, pay cash, and do not have a receipt issued in your own name. Make up a name, if you need it."

"I assume I have also not been to London today?"

"An excellent assumption."

"What was I doing, instead?"

"You remember our picnic lunch down by the airstrip?"

"Of course."

"That was today, not yesterday. You may say that I kept you fully occupied for that time."

"By 'fully occupied,' you mean . . ."

"Use your imagination. We may have frightened the horses."

"I notice that you have booked the suite for two nights. Will we take advantage of that?"

"That remains to be seen. Now that you mention it, what you have in mind might make a good alibi, if we don't have the linen changed."

"A lot of fun, too. I'm still all rosy from last night."

"And the night before, I expect."

"Well, yes. I don't often participate in that particular activity, but it certainly makes an interesting change."

"I will not take that statement amiss."

"Nor should you," she said, kissing him on the ear.

"Fasten your seat belt," Stone said. "We don't want to start anything we can't finish in the front seat of a Porsche."

43

Stone dropped Tara at the Knightsbridge entrance to the Harvey Nichols store, then drove around Hyde Park Corner, up Piccadilly, down to Trafalgar Square, and into the Strand. He turned into the Savoy Hotel driveway and gave his car to a valet. As he got out of the Porsche, he was approached by a young man he didn't know. Stone put his hand under his jacket, where his pistol lived.

"Easy. I'm Jeffers," the young man said.

Stone relaxed.

Jeffers handed him an envelope. "Here are your key cards. You are registered under the names of Mr. and Mrs. John Withers, though I don't see a Mrs. Withers here."

"She'll be along later," Stone said.

"I'll park myself in a little cubbyhole outside

the Oscar Wilde suite. Shout out should you require assistance. I assume you have a firearm?"

"I do. A small 9mm."

"Is it equipped for a silencer?"

"It will accept one, but I am not so equipped."

Jeffers slipped something heavy into Stone's coat pocket. "You may keep this. It has no identification marks." He pressed a box into Stone's hand. "This is a listening device, which can be held against a wall or door, amplifying sound from the other side. You may keep this, too. It is custom-made and carries no markings. There is also a paper surgical mask inside, which might come in useful for not being recognized."

"Thank you, Jeffers." Stone made his way into the hotel and down a ground-floor hallway to the end, where the Oscar Wilde suite lay. There was a DO NOT DISTURB sign hanging on the doorknob. He went next door to the Gilbert & Sullivan suite, let himself in, and had a good look around. It was beautifully furnished and had two large windows in the living room, overlooking the River Thames, with a park in between.

Stone set down the box he had been given and the silencer beside it. He screwed the silencer into the barrel of the pistol; a perfect fit. He opened the box and found an unmarked black box. He flipped a switch on the side, held it to the door between the adjoining suites, and pressed his ear against the other side. He heard the sound of a man turning over in bed, and a sort of snort. The box did a beautiful job of amplifying.

Stone inspected his pistol to be sure it was loaded. He pumped one up the snout and switched on the safety. He listened again at the door and heard nothing. Slowly, he turned the lock on his side of the door, turned the knob, and pushed. The door opened an inch. He still heard nothing.

He opened the door enough to allow him to enter, closing it silently behind him. As an afterthought, he slipped on the surgical mask and adjusted it for easy breathing, then he slipped off his shoes and walked down a short hallway to an open door. He looked inside and saw an empty bed with the covers pushed back. There was no one in the room.

Then he heard a clearing of the throat, apparently coming from the open bathroom door on the other side of the bed. He walked around the bed, then peeked carefully into the bathroom. A man sat on the toilet facing him, his pajama bottoms around his ankles. Stone stepped around the doorjamb, the pistol held out in front of him, pointed at the man's head. The man's jaw dropped, but Stone remembered him from Caravaggio. It was Trafficante.

"Shut up and sit still," Stone said to him.

Trafficante froze and held out his hands, as if to ward off an evil spirit.

"I believe I have you at a disadvantage," Stone said. "My name is Barrington, and I believe that I have just demonstrated to you that I can find you anywhere in the world and kill you, if I so choose. Do you agree?"

Trafficante nodded. "Yes," he said, his voice hoarse. He cleared his throat again.

"First, I have some information for you," Stone said. "My brief relationship with Hilda Ross had nothing to do with you. I did not know that you existed at the time. Now you are engaged in an insane attempt to murder me, apparently out of jealousy. Is that correct?"

Trafficante let his gaze drop, as if he didn't want to answer.

"Would you like me to shoot you in the knee to gain your undivided attention?"

"No," Trafficante said. "Please don't do that."

"If anyone, for any reason, makes an attempt to harm me, I am going to assume that he has been instructed by you, do you understand?"

Trafficante nodded. "Yes, I understand. You will have no further trouble from me."

"I could doubt your word and shoot you in both knees now, just to prove that I can."

"Please, don't do that. I give you my word you will have no further trouble."

"Good. Remember, I can find you anywhere and kill or cripple you at will."

"I will remember."

"Sit there for five minutes before you move again," Stone said. He stepped out of the bathroom, walked across the bedroom, down the hall, and locked the door to the adjoining suite, then let himself out the front door and closed it behind him, turning over the card on the doorknob to read, SERVICE, PLEASE. It wouldn't hurt Trafficante to have another unexpected visitor.

He let himself into the Gilbert & Sullivan suite, picked up the phone, and ordered lunch.

Stone had eaten his lunch and was having a nap on the bed when his cell phone rang. "Yes?"

"It's Jeffers. Mr. T. has checked out of the hotel. The doorman tells me a car was waiting to take him to RAF Northam, a military base to the west of London that also accepts corporate aircraft. I have a man following him, and I will be in touch."

"Excellent."

"By the way, I don't know what went on in there, but you apparently scared the shit out of him. He looked terrible."

"I'm glad to hear it." Stone hung up.

Less than an hour later, the cell rang again. "Yes?"

"It's Jeffers. Mr. T. has boarded a corporate jet and has taken off. The pilot filed for Teterboro,

New Jersey, flight time about seven hours. He has a bit of a headwind today."

"Thank you once again, Mr. Jeffers. I shall let Dame Felicity know that your work was outstanding."

"Thank you, sir, anytime." Jeffers hung up.

Stone called Tara's cell.

"Hello, there!"

"Are you all shopped out?"

"Not quite."

"Dinner at the Savoy this evening?"

"Yes, please."

"When you're done, take a cab to the Savoy. We're in the Gilbert & Sullivan suite. The subject of our interest has checked out and fled for New York."

"Oh, good. Another hour?"

"Fine." They both hung up.

44

They left the Savoy the following day at mid-morning, after reading a note from the front desk, addressed to Mr. and Mrs. Withers, that their bill had already been settled. The trunk of the Porsche was filled with shopping bags, and the two rear seats—apparently intended for legless children—were jammed, too.

They had finished lunch at Windward Hall, and most of the group were napping, when Stone, sitting in the library, got a cell phone call. The caller ID read: **Private**. "Yes?"

"What did you do to him?" a female voice asked.

"What?"

"He got in around midnight and immediately beat the shit out of me. I'll have to have a professional makeup artist in today so I can work my closing show tonight at the Carlyle. And I have to see a dentist to have a temporary crown installed to plug a gap."

"Hilda," Stone said, "you should start being more discriminating in your choice of male company."

"It's a little late for that," she said. "He's insanely possessive. He'll never let me go."

"If you want to run and hide, I'll help."

"Where are you?"

"I left London this morning, outward bound."

"Still on the other side of the Atlantic?"

"That's a possibility."

"Why are you being so cagey with me?"

"Because the last time I trusted you, I found your boyfriend on my tail. Do you blame me?"

She ignored that. "You said you could help me run. Run where?"

"I have a house in Maine with caretakers. The caretakers can make you comfortable."

"How do I get there?"

"Rent a car. It's an eight-hour drive and a ten-minute ferry ride."

"Suppose he knows about that house?"

"If he thinks I'm there he won't intrude, believe me. Our meeting yesterday frightened him badly."

"And he took it out on me."

"You have only yourself to blame."

"Will you be going to Maine?"

"No. I'll be occupied elsewhere."

"You mean you're fucking someone else."

"So are you."

"How long can I stay there?"

"Up to you. Stay until you feel safe going elsewhere."

"I'm not a very good driver. I don't like driving long distances."

"I also have a house in Key West. There are nonstop flights. And the potatoes are too small there to attract goombahs."

"Is it private?"

"Yes, and you need never leave the house. The housekeeper will see to your meals."

"I don't know what to do."

"Figure it out." Stone hung up.

Dino came into the library.

"No nap?"

"I couldn't sleep, worrying about you."

Stone laughed. "I'll bet."

"How did it go yesterday?"

"Let's just say that Mr. Trafficante and I met yesterday and came to terms."

"You reasoned with him? He doesn't seem like that kind of guy."

"I think it helped that I had a silenced pistol pointed at his head, which made him more reasonable. It didn't hurt, either, that he was on the toilet with his pants around his ankles. I think that made him feel more vulnerable. Also, now he believes I can find him anywhere."

"That's good news."

"Unfortunately, when he got home, he took it out on Hilda. She was on the phone a minute ago, complaining about being beaten up."

"Why doesn't she just get out?"

"She has one more performance at the Carlyle. After that, I've offered her either the Maine or the Key West house."

"You didn't offer her the L.A. place at the Arrington?"

"I don't want her to get too comfortable; she might not want to leave."

"Good point. Did she take you up on the offer?"

"She'll think about it and let me know."

As if on cue, Stone's cell phone rang.

"Yes?"

"All right, Key West."

Stone gave her the address. "Take a cab. I'll let the housekeeper know you're coming."

"How will I amuse myself?"

"There are books and TV. If you get bored, there's always autoeroticism. But I wouldn't go looking for companionship; you might be spotted."

"So I have to be imprisoned the whole time."

"You can do whatever you damned well please,"

Stone said, "but don't get blood or brains on the furniture. Goodbye." He hung up.

Dino was laughing. "I'll bet she doesn't get many invitations like that one."

"I think we can safely return to New York now," Stone said. "How about we have dinner at the Squadron tonight and take off around eleven tomorrow morning? That'll get us home from Teterboro before rush hour."

"Sounds good," Dino said.

Viv and Tara came into the room. "What's the plan?" Viv asked.

"Go back upstairs and change for a black-tie dinner; we're dining at the Royal Yacht Squadron, departing our dock at five-thirty. Tomorrow, wheels up at eleven AM for New York."

"Is it safe now?"

"As safe as I know how to make it," Stone replied. He called the Key West housekeeper, then Faith, explained their travel plans, then went upstairs to change for dinner.

At a little after six o'clock, Stone docked the boat at the little marina next to the Squadron, and they walked up to the castle. Stone gave Tara the tour, then they all sat down for drinks.

Stone was sipping from the supply of Knob Creek he had bestowed to the club, when his cell phone rang, ID: **Private.** He stepped out onto the terrace, where the view was of a group of yachts maneuvering for the start of a race.

"Yes?"

"It's Hilda."

"Now what?"

"Sal just called. He wants me to go to Florida with him tomorrow morning."

"Why are you telling me this?"

"I thought you might have a suggestion," she said.

"I do," Stone replied. "Handle it." He hung up and went back inside.

45

Stone asked Faith, on takeoff, to make a low, 360-degree turn over the estate, so they could have a last look at Windward Hall. Stone wanted that stamped on his frontal lobe until his next visit.

They set down at Teterboro in the early afternoon and were towed into the hangar before deplaning and transferring their luggage.

"Stone," Tara said, "as fond as I've become of your living arrangements, I would like to stop by Bucks County, Pennsylvania, and spend a couple of days confirming that my employees have not fled with the equipment and stock and that they are still printing money in the basement."

"Take all the time you need," Stone said. "I

need a little time to recover my health before I see you again."

"You're sweet," she said, kissing him.

Stone arrived at home and, since he didn't have any luggage, except his briefcase, went straight upstairs. As he got off the elevator and started down the hallway to the master suite, he stopped in his tracks. Someone had left a light on in there. He knew it had not been he, nor did he believe the maids would have done that.

He unholstered his pistol and started down the hall. As he approached, he heard a noise, unidentified but of human origin, he was sure. He entered the bedroom slowly, his gun at the ready, and he was shaken to see Hilda Ross coming out of the dressing room. She jumped when she saw him with a gun.

"Where is he?" Stone said.

"Sal? Not here," she said, bending to set down a train case, which involved revealing a lot of cleavage. "Nobody here but us chickens. Want to do something about that?"

Stone reckoned there were two choices: the first, to shoot her. He elected for the second option. She was out of her dress before he reached her. And before he could ask himself what the hell he was doing, they were doing it. No words were exchanged, just noises.

They explored much of the erotic repertoire. When they were done, lying there weak and panting, she said, "I hadn't expected that."

"Neither had I," Stone said. "I had expected to be shooting Sal."

"Don't worry, he's on his way to Florida."

"Where were you on the way to, when you broke into my house?"

"You gave me a key, remember?"

"I do not."

"And the alarm code." She repeated it.

"Okay, I gave them both to you. What are your plans?"

"After I've fucked you at least once more, I'm going to the Carlyle and surrender to the makeup artist." She smiled. "The tooth's already done, see? Then I'm packing up and getting an early-morning flight to Key West. Care to come with me?"

"We just did that."

She took hold of his wrist and checked his pulse. "And after this returns to normal, we'll do it again, with variations."

"You think I can still do that?"

"I know you can, from experience. It's one of the things I like best about you." She fondled him lightly. "See?"

Stone was too tired to argue with her.

* * *

A couple of hours later, she tucked him in. "I'll call you from Key West," she said. "Maybe I can persuade you to come there."

"I may never come again," he said. Then, to his overwhelming relief, she was gone.

Stone slept until mid-evening, when Dino called.

"Hello."

"You sound exhausted," Dino said.

"I am as I sound."

"But you dropped off Tara."

"I did."

"Then . . . Oh, no, not Hilda."

"She was here when I arrived, and she waylaid me."

"By arrangement?"

"Not by my arrangement."

"Where's Sal?"

"On his way to Florida, she said. She's leaving for Key West tomorrow morning."

"Is the state big enough for both of them?"

"Apparently so."

"You're not going down there, are you?"

"If I did, I might not get out alive."

"I told you she could be fatal."

"I think you're right, but she's using a different arsenal of weapons than you predicted."

"I'll let you get back to sleep. You need it." Dino hung up, and Stone went back to sleep.

46

Jack Coulter walked out onto his terrace overlooking Central Park, wet a finger, and held it up to judge the breeze. Almost none. The sun shone brightly; it was an inviting day.

He left the building and set out at a brisk walk for the Brook, his favorite club. Fifteen minutes later he was being seated alone at a table in the rapidly filling dining room. Five minutes after that, the head of the Mafia on the East Coast of the United States and his consigliere were seated not five feet from him. It took only a glance to recognize Don Antonio Datilla and Sal Trafficante, before they noticed him, and by then he was deeply into the menu.

They discussed the food in English, ordered. Then, after checking out Jack thoroughly and finding him to be an upper-class white man of no interest to him, nor they to him, slipped into their Sicilian dialect.

"So Hilda's back?" the Don said.

"Yeah," Sal replied. "I gave her a good going over to keep her honest, but not enough to make her look bad on stage tonight. I couldn't stretch her booking; last night was her last performance at the Carlyle."

"What will you do with her next? She's a very useful person, I have found. She kills without batting an eye."

"We'll see," Sal replied.

"Barrington?"

"I can't let myself be seen by that gentleman."

Coulter, who had been getting bored, sat up a little straighter.

"Why not?" the Don asked.

"We had an encounter in London."

"What was Barrington doing in London when Hilda was here?"

"I think he was looking for me. He came into my hotel suite with a gun."

"Why didn't you kill him?"

"Two reasons: It's messy to kill abroad; our friends are fewer there. The other is that I was in my pajamas, with no weapon handy."

"I cannot imagine you without a weapon handy," the Don said.

"In a suite at the Savoy?"

"Let that be a lesson."

"Oh, yes, but it makes it difficult, if not impossible, to approach Barrington. He knows me now."

"Where is Hilda now?"

"On her way to Key West, Florida."

"Why there?"

"Because Barrington has offered her his house there, to keep her safe from me."

The Don digested this for a moment. "Will Barrington visit her there?"

"Her allure is such that I think he might find that an irresistible idea," Sal said.

"Ideal," the Don said. "She can kill him there and walk away. No one there knows her, right?"

"Right."

"She finds him attractive. Will she have the guts to do it?"

"Her guts can be purchased."

"For how much?"

"First, she has to lure him there," Sal said "Once she's inside his head, he'll do whatever she desires."

"She's that good in bed, eh?"

"Better than anyone could imagine."

"If I were younger, I'd try her on for size."

"You would not be disappointed," Sal said.

"Would you like me to arrange a trip to Key West for you?"

The Don held up both hands. "No, no. I'd never be able to explain it to my wife. Besides, I'm not sure my heart could stand it."

"Yes, but what a way to go!"

The two men laughed heartily.

Coulter's soup came and he drank it slowly.

"You didn't tell me how much she'd cost," the Don said.

"We paid her fifty grand to do Manny Fiore."

"Ouch! Are you going to tell me she'll cost a hundred grand?"

"She felt nothing for Manny, but she'll have some scruples to overcome with Barrington."

"Scruples are expensive."

"Exactly.

"All right, a hundred grand—for you. I wouldn't do that for anyone else."

"Thank you, Don Antonio. I will be eternally grateful. I wish I could get close enough to do it myself. I'd like to watch him die."

Coulter finished his lunch and watched them depart as he had his dessert. Those two would never dream that someone at the Brook would have understood their conversation. He gave them time enough to drive away, then he signed his check and went looking for a cab.

* * *

Stone was finishing a sandwich at his desk and feeling a little sore. It amazed him that he could still be aroused just by thinking about Hilda and what they had done the afternoon before. It was disturbing, too.

He jumped as his cell phone rang. "Yes?"

"I just got in and got settled," Hilda said. "I'm lying on your bed, thinking about yesterday."

"A pity you're so far away."

"You're the one who's far away," she said. "Why don't you come and visit me here? The weather is lovely."

"It's not so bad here," he said.

"Do you know what I would like to do to you, if you were here?"

"Don't tell me."

She told him.

"Stop it."

"Are you getting, ah, interested?"

"Who wouldn't?"

"Good, that's a start. Let me see what else I can think of."

"Please don't."

She thought of something.

"I have to go now."

"No, you have to come now."

"I'd need you for that."

"I'm right here," she said. "Come tomorrow."

"I'll see what I can do," Stone said.

"We both already know what you can do," she said. "Just do it here."

"I'll think about it," Stone said, then hung up.

He was thinking about it! Was he crazy?

47

Stone had just hung up when Joan buzzed. "Jack Coulter is here. He doesn't have an appointment."

"Send him in."

Jack came in, waved, and sat down.

"You look like a man in a hurry," Stone said.

"I was afraid you'd already be dead," Jack said.

"Don't rush me."

"Do you know who Antonio Datilla is?"

"The Don?"

"Correct."

"How about Salvatore Trafficante?"

"The Don's consigliere."

"You're better informed than I thought," Jack said.

"It sounds as if you want to inform me further."

"I just had lunch at the Brook, and they were sitting closer to me than you are now."

"Tell me more."

"They were speaking Sicilian, not knowing that I grew up in a household with a grandmother who spoke nothing else."

"So you eavesdropped?"

"Didn't bat an eyelid. You'd have been proud of me."

"What was the content of their conversation?"

"Mostly you and a woman named Hilda, who, I understand, is in residence at your Key West house."

"You understand way too much," Stone said. "She wasn't supposed to tell anybody."

"That's when some women tell everybody," Jack pointed out.

"Not Hilda, not everybody. Just the guy who wants me dead."

"They're going to offer her a hundred thousand dollars to do it. You should be flattered. The last time she killed for them they only paid fifty thousand." Jack leaned forward. "You're thinking about fucking her again, aren't you."

"How did you know that?"

"You're attracted by the idea of doing that to her before she can do the other thing to you."

"If I'm not blushing, I should be," Stone said.

"Don't do it, Stone. That's a fool's bet."

"I can't disagree with you," Stone said.

"Tell you what. Why don't I go down there and kill her for you?"

"If you met her, you'd want to fuck her first," Stone said.

"I suppose there's a bit of a challenge involved."

"It's a nice thought, Jack, and I appreciate it, but you don't want to get involved in this."

"What about you?"

"I'm already involved. If I don't go down to Key West, she'll come up here."

"She won't be expecting me."

"Don't underestimate her, Jack."

"Then let me find another assassin—one who won't be tempted to fuck her first."

"What kind of assassin is that?"

"A woman."

Stone thought about that. "Possibly."

"Certainly."

"How can you be sure the woman won't want to fuck her, too?"

"Because she's cold-blooded and coldhearted. She doesn't let anything get in the way of business, not even sex."

"Interesting."

"And she's already in Florida."

"Where?"

"Palm Beach."

"How much?" Stone suddenly realized that he was talking about sending a hired killer to murder someone.

"Twenty-five grand," Jack said.

"Sounds cheap, for that line of business."

"It's a discount for me."

"Why for you?"

"Because I got her out of a very bad jam, once. Saved her life. She's pitifully grateful."

"I thought you said she was cold-blooded and coldhearted."

"Not where I'm concerned."

Stone thought some more.

"Don't let your conscience get the better of you, Stone. Hilda is taking money to kill you. That should let you see just where you stand on her list of priorities."

"This can't happen in my house," Stone said. "It's a small town."

"Then we'll have to arrange for the deed to be done somewhere else."

"Is your lady smart enough to handle that?"

"It's what she does," Jack said. "And she's never been caught, or even suspected."

"Why don't you have a chat with her and see what's involved? And I want to know everything: how she gets to Key West from Palm Beach, how she gets back, how she deals with the body, how she covers her tracks. What is your lady's name?"

"Gigi."

"What else?"

"Just Gigi."

"Is she beautiful?"

"Just a sec," Jack said. He got out an iPhone and started scrolling, then stopped and handed the phone to Stone.

Tall, slim, looked great in the bikini. "Wow."

"Will she appeal to Hilda?"

"E-mail this to me, and we'll find out," Stone said.

Jack e-mailed the photo.

"We'd better give Gigi another name," Stone said.

"Why?"

"If they travel in the same crowd, Hilda could have heard of her."

"All right: Cara," Jack said. "Cara Connery." He stared off into space.

"Are you having second thoughts, Jack?"

"Always," Jack replied. "That's how you stay ahead of the game."

48

Stone called Hilda's throwaway.

"Well, hi, there," she breathed, making the hair on Stone's chest stand on end. "Are you on your way?"

"Not for a couple of days. Complications at the law firm. I'll be there, though."

"You'd better hurry. I might explode."

"It occurred to me that I could send you a playmate to keep you busy, until I get there."

"Who is he?" She sounded doubtful, even a little hurt.

"She, not he. Her name is Cara Connery. A year or so ago, I offered her the house, but the timing was wrong. She called today and said she'd like to go down."

"That part sounds interesting. How did you know I like a girl now and then?"

"Intuition," Stone said. "Hang on, I'll send you a photo." He sent it on its way. "Got it?"

"Yes, and I want it."

"Let me call her and tell her about you, then I'll get right back." He hung up.

"Did she bite?" Jack asked.

"Oh, yes. You'd better call Cara." He explained what he'd told Hilda.

"I've already spoken to Cara, while you were on the phone."

"What was her reaction?"

"Positive," Jack said. "Enthusiastic when I offered her twenty-five grand and expenses."

"She knows why she's going, then?"

"Yes."

"She knows not to be seen with Hilda or to leave a body in my house?"

"Disposal is included. Cara will drop her off in the Everglades on her way home, in the dead of night. There are hungry things in the Everglades."

Stone sat and stared at his desk. How was this any different from killing Trafficante at the Savoy? He had been ready to do that, he thought.

"You're still going to have to deal with Trafficante, though. From his conversation with his Don, I'd say he hates you."

"Believe me, I realize that."

"I may be able to help with that, too."

"I may **need** help with that." Stone buzzed Joan. "How much cash do we have in the safe?"

"About thirty-five thousand, I think."

"Put twenty-five of it into an envelope and bring it to me, please." He turned to Jack. "Where is Cara now?"

"In New York, for a few days' shopping."

"I think she'd better get to Key West right away, before Hilda gets bored again. She can rent a car at the airport and return it in Palm Beach."

"She'll be on a six o'clock plane. Should be at your house by nine."

Joan came in with a fat envelope. "Give it to Mr. Coulter, please. He's going to make an investment for me."

Joan gave Jack the envelope. "Do we need a receipt?" she asked Stone.

"That won't be necessary," Stone replied. "Restock, though."

"Will do." Joan left.

"Tell Cara that the maid is off this week. She'll be back on Monday to clean up after Hilda."

"That's convenient," Jack said.

Stone gave him the address and directions to the house from the airport, and the code for the driveway gate. "Tell her there's off-street parking, and she can use the garage closest to the house; same gate code."

"Do you want her to call you when it's done?"

"No, I want her to call **you** when it's done.

Then you can call me and just say 'the package arrived,' and I'll know she's on her way back to Palm Beach."

"Done," Jack said, rising. "I've got to get home. Hillary and I are dining with friends tonight."

"Thank you, Jack," Stone said, and saw him out.

Stone went back to his desk and called Hilda.

"What's up?"

"Cara," Stone said. "She's landing this evening; should be at the house by nine. She's got this number, if she needs to reach you."

"I'm looking forward to it," Hilda said.

"I'll be down the day after tomorrow. I'll let you know what time to expect me."

"My guess is, you can expect to find both Cara and me here," Hilda said. "We'll plan something special for you."

"That sounds enticing," Stone said. They both hung up.

The phone rang, making Stone jump.

"Hello?"

"It's Dino. What's up?"

"Not much."

"Dinner at P.J.'s, seven o'clock?"

"You're on." Stone hung up. He'd need the alibi.

49

Stone and Dino met at the bar, as usual, then half a drink later, asked for their table. They settled in and ordered.

Dino looked at Stone. "What's wrong?" he asked.

"Wrong?"

"Come on, Stone. You can't hide it from me."

"Hide what from you?"

"You're planning to do something you think I wouldn't like."

"That's a wild guess," Stone replied.

"But a good one."

Stone shrugged.

"Why would you hide it from me?"

"Let me ask you a hypothetical question."

"Okay, shoot."

"Suppose, for a moment, that I was planning to do something illegal. Would you want to know?"

Dino drew a big breath. "How illegal?"

"'Against the law' illegal. I know you'd try to talk me out of it, but what if you couldn't?"

"Huh?"

"What if you couldn't talk me out of it? Would you arrest me?"

"I think I have it," Dino said.

"Go ahead, guess."

"You're planning to kill Sal Trafficante, aren't you?"

"No, but if he keeps trying to kill me, it may come to that."

"Is he trying to kill you now?"

"Yes."

"Then let me put some people on it."

"It's in another state."

"Florida?"

"I won't be specific."

"Hilda is in Florida. Is she involved in this?"

"She's awfully anxious for me to come to Key West."

"Then don't go there."

"If I don't, she'll find another way. She may even come here to do it. Then I won't see her coming."

"Okay, I see what's eating you now. You don't want me to know what you're planning."

"It's for your own benefit. No reason you should have to share the burden."

"Look. If you and Hilda and I were in the same

room, and I thought she was going to try to kill you, I'd kill her."

"Well, she is going to try. Would you send somebody from New York to take her out before she could take me out?"

"That's an impossible situation for me."

"That's why I'm not involving you, Dino. What you don't know can't hurt you."

Dino shut up and looked around the room. "Is anybody in this room involved?"

Stone looked around. "No."

"So nobody can be listening to us?"

"I'm not wearing a wire, Dino."

"All right, I'll go down there and kill her myself," Dino said.

Stone's jaw dropped, and he started laughing.

"What? You think I'm kidding?"

"I know you're not kidding, and I love you for it. Listen to me: the best thing you can do for me right now is to forget about this. Put it right out of your mind, and don't bring it up again. But I don't know if you're capable of that."

"Of course, I'm capable of that."

"Capable of what?"

"What you just said."

"I don't remember saying anything. What are you talking about, Dino?"

Dino leaned in close. "Offing two people."

"What are you talking about? Why would I want to do that?"

"You just said . . ." Dino stopped. "All right, I get it."

"Get what?"

"I'll stay out of it."

"Stay out of what?"

"Whatever you're doing."

"Doing? What am I doing?"

"Whatever you want to, and with no interference from me."

"Sometimes I think you're completely crazy," Stone said.

"Sometimes I think so, too."

They talked about other things.

Jack Coulter's throwaway buzzed in his pocket. "Excuse me for a moment," he said to Hillary. He left the table and walked around a corner. "Yeah?"

"I'm leaving the airport," she said. "I'll be at the house in ten minutes."

"Everything okay?"

"I'm all set."

"Call me as planned."

"Sure."

They both hung up.

Cara, as she had begun to think of herself, followed the GPS directions to the house and drove up to the keypad and entered the code. The gate swung open, and the garage ahead of her was empty. She drove in, got her bag from the trunk, and rang the bell.

A smiling woman opened the door. "Cara?"

"And you're Hilda."

"I am. Come on in, and let me get you a drink." She led Cara to the bar. "The photo Stone sent me doesn't do you justice."

"Thank you," Cara said, with a big smile.

"What would you like?"

"That's a leading question, but let's start with a Scotch on the rocks. Chivas, if you have it."

"We have it." Hilda poured them both a drink.

"Beautiful place," Cara said, looking around.

"I'll give you the tour." She did so, then they returned to the bar and Hilda poured another drink for them both. "Oh, I didn't show you the master bedroom, did I?"

"No, you didn't, but I'd like to see it." She picked up her bag and her drink and followed Hilda down to the end of the main hall, where Hilda opened the door.

"Ah, nice," Cara said, dropping her bag and sitting on the bed.

Hilda sat next to her. "You're a beautiful girl," she said.

"So are you," Cara replied, bending and kissing her on her bare shoulder. "I think I'd like a shower after my trip," she said.

"Would you like me to join you?" Hilda asked.

"I'd love that." She undressed and walked into the bathroom.

"Be right with you," Hilda called out and got undressed. She bent and unzipped Cara's Vuitton bag and moved the clothes aside. At the bottom were a silenced pistol and a switchblade knife. She zipped it up, then went into the bathroom, where Cara was already in the shower.

They kissed, then Cara dragged over a stool from a corner and sat Hilda down. Cara knelt and buried her face in Hilda's lap.

Hilda allowed herself to enjoy it to the point of orgasm, then she reached up to the shelf beside her, behind a row of bottles, and removed a kitchen implement.

Timing her orgasm with her move, she ran her fingers up Cara's spine until she found the right spot, then in one swift move, plunged the ice pick into her back and her heart. She stood and backed away from Cara, taking the ice pick with her. Cara was on her hands and knees, trying to get up, but she couldn't make it.

With the ice pick at the ready, should she need it again, Hilda watched Cara finally collapse to the tiled floor. She turned her over to allow her to bleed out faster. It took no more than half a minute.

Hilda left her to drain for another minute, then turned off the shower, got out and dried herself.

She went back into the bedroom and searched Cara's bag more thoroughly, finding bundles of hundred-dollar bills.

Hilda made herself some dinner and poured a glass of wine, thinking about what she would shop for with Cara's money. She regretted not keeping her alive long enough to learn who had paid her, but there were only two candidates: Sal and Stone Barrington. She wouldn't have thought Stone had the kind of guts it took to hire a killer, and pay for the job, but it was he who'd sent Cara down. It had to be Stone.

When she had finished dinner, she rummaged in the garage and found some plastic sheeting and a roll of duct tape. She went back to the bathroom and dragged Cara's body out of the shower and onto the plastic sheeting, then wrapped her and taped the bundle securely. She checked the shower to be sure that all of the blood had run down the drain, then she laid down a large bath towel and dragged her into the bedroom. She found Cara's car keys, then dragged the body down the hall and into the garage. She opened the trunk and, with considerable effort, got the body inside and closed it.

She looked inside and found a rental car agreement: Cara had picked up the car at the Key West airport and was returning it at the Palm Beach airport. She found the rental car map and looked at the drive: seven or eight hours, she reckoned, and her route took her along Alligator Alley, through the Everglades. Cara could take her final dip there.

Hilda packed her bags, then had a cup of coffee to keep her awake. After a final check of the house to be sure that it was clean of any trace of Cara, she tossed Cara's bag into the car with her own, then got into the rental, closed the garage door and the gate behind her, and headed up the Keys.

50

Jack Coulter lay in his bed and stared at the ceiling. The bedside clock showed 2:45 AM, and he was trying to think of a reason why Cara hadn't called. He thought of calling Stone, but what could he do? He'd just have to wait until morning. And try to sleep.

Hilda drove up the Keys to Key Largo, then turned north and made her way into the Everglades. The moon was bright enough that she could drive with only her side lights on. Somewhere north, she found a dirt road snaking off to her left. She turned on her headlights and drove slowly until she came to a shack on a river. It sported a sign: LIVE BAIT, and there was a dock beside it where a couple of small boats were moored. She got a small but powerful flashlight from her bag and played it over the water. It was tidal, and the tide was coming in.

She dragged Cara's body from the car out onto the dock, then sat and rested for a moment. Next, she ripped off the duct tape, wadded it, and threw it into the water, watching it float upriver with the tide. Finally, she dragged the body to the edge of the dock and rolled it into the water. It went under for a moment, then floated to the top. When it emerged, it was a few feet upstream, then it kept going. Hilda heard a couple of splashes from farther up, then some thrashing.

She then carefully folded the plastic sheeting, found some stacked bricks beside the shed, put three of them into Cara's bag, and tossed it into the water. She got back into the car and retraced her steps to U.S. 1. After she had passed Cutler Bay, she stopped at a convenience store, used the restroom, then filled up with gas. While the pump was running she took the folded plastic sheeting from the trunk and deposited it in the trash can. Then she was on her way to the Florida Turnpike, thence to West Palm Beach and the airport. She turned in the rental car, paid cash. Then she booked herself on the next flight to New York and had some breakfast, thinking about shopping.

* * *

Stone was awakened early by his ringing phone. Dino, he reckoned. "Good morning."

"Good morning, Stone, it's Jack Coulter."

"Oh, hello, Jack."

"There's a problem."

"What?"

"Our girl didn't phone last night. I tried her this morning, but it went straight to voicemail."

Stone was quiet for a moment.

"Have you heard from her or from Hilda?"

"No, neither."

"I don't think there's anything more we can do until we hear from one of them," Jack said.

"I agree."

"Let's talk after we get a call."

They both hung up.

Stone spent his usual morning at his desk, then around noon, his cell phone rang. "Hello?"

"Hi, it's Hilda."

"Good morning. Did you and Cara have a pleasant evening?"

"She never showed. I was disappointed. Has she called you?"

"No, I've heard nothing," Stone said.

"I took a morning flight to New York. Would you like to get together?"

"No, I can't, until tomorrow."

"Tomorrow night, then?"

"Sure. What's your number?"

"I've got a new throwaway." She gave him the number.

"Are you going to see Sal while you're here?"

"I don't know. I don't particularly want to."

"All right. Where are you staying?"

"At the Carlyle. They give me the rack rate for a suite."

"I'll pick you up at the Seventy-Sixth Street entrance at seven, then."

"Good. We can come back to the Carlyle later."

"Great. Bye."

Stone hung up and called Jack.

"Hello, Stone."

"I just had a call from Hilda. She said that Cara never showed. Hilda's in New York now. We made a date for tomorrow night."

"I wouldn't keep it, if I were you. If Hilda's alive, that tells you she knows everything."

"That thought didn't occur to me."

"Look at it this way: you've got two women who met last night, both of whom are contract killers, and one of them is missing."

"You have a point," Stone said.

"I figure Cara made a move, but Hilda got there first. Now Hilda is going to be wondering who sent her."

"Well, yes."

"I don't think you would survive another session in bed with Hilda."

Stone gulped.

"Do you know where Hilda is staying?"

"In a suite at the Carlyle."

"That's a little expensive for a single person, isn't it?"

"She performs there sometimes. She says they give her a rate."

"Of course. And if I'm thinking correctly, she'll have your twenty-five thousand dollars."

"Yes, I suppose."

"I think your next move should be out of town," Jack said.

"I'll think about that," Stone replied.

"Let's talk when you've figured out your next move."

"Good." They both hung up.

Stone called Dino.

"Bacchetti."

"We need to talk," Stone said, "and not on the phone."

"What's up?"

"I need some advice. Dinner at Patroon, seven o'clock?"

"Okay. Viv's out of town."

"Good."

Stone hung up, relieved. He didn't want to explain any of this to Viv.

He tried to put himself in Hilda's position. What would she do next? If he didn't show for dinner tomorrow night, she'd smell a rat, and that would be him.

Maybe he should talk to Jack again, before it came to that. Jack seemed to be full of ideas, even if the last one hadn't worked so well.

51

Stone arrived before Dino, and the waiter automatically brought him a Knob Creek. He looked around the room and saw one or two people he knew, but no one of consequence. Then he was startled to find Dino at his elbow.

Dino sat down. "You look even worse than the last time I saw you," he said.

"That's because things are worse."

"Did you have Hilda dealt with?"

"A friend of mine has a friend, who does that sort of work. It was arranged for the two of them to meet at the Key West house. She was supposed to call my friend when the work was finished."

"And she didn't call?"

"No, and she's not answering her phone, either. I spoke to Hilda, and she said the woman never showed."

Dino thought about that for a minute. "Where do murderers in Key West dispose of bodies?"

"I have no idea."

"You read the local paper when you're there. They publish that sort of information."

"In the water, I guess. It's an island. It's surrounded by water."

Dino got out his cell phone. "What's the name of the newspaper?"

"The **Key West Citizen**. A body in the water would make the front page, and the story would be continued on the last page."

Dino went to work with his thumbs. "Nothing," he said. "How about a newspaper with a wider coverage?"

"Miami, I guess. The **Herald**?"

Dino typed some more, then he stopped. "Uh-oh."

"What?"

Dino started scrolling down. "Parts of a woman's body were found up a creek in the Everglades."

"Which parts?"

"It doesn't say, just that they belonged to a whole woman at some point."

"Are they thinking alligators?"

"From what I hear, gators are very helpful when it comes to converting bodies into body parts."

"Well, she can be identified with DNA," Stone said.

"You got any DNA?"

"No, I've never met her." He dug out his iPhone and found the photo.

"Hey, nice body parts!" Dino said. "A shame to rearrange them."

Stone called Jack. "Google the **Miami Herald** front page," he said.

"Give me a minute," Jack responded, then he came back. "Can you zoom in close on what looks like a left hand?"

"I'll try." Stone enlarged the **Herald** photo. "Looks like a little gold ring on the pinkie."

"Now do the same with the photo I sent you."

Stone managed the operation. "I can't get any real detail, but they're both small and gold and on the same finger."

"Cara, let's call her, wore a little gold signet ring on that finger. She said Tiffany's had it made for her; a family crest."

"Probably not a coincidence, huh?"

"Do you know anybody at the **Herald**?" Jack asked.

"The only **name** I know at the **Herald** is Carl Hiaasen, a columnist, but I've never met him. I do read his books."

"I'll see if I can find a way to get an anonymous note to the editor," Jack said. "I'll call you if I have any luck." He hung up.

"So?" Dino asked.

Stone showed him the two rings.

"You shoulda been a Detective," Dino said.

"Do you think you could find a way to tip off the Miami cops without getting either of us dragged into it?"

"Maybe."

"It could help that the ring is supposed to have been made by Tiffany's; a family crest."

"What's the woman's name?"

"If I knew her real name, I've forgotten it."

Dino made a brief call to somebody he knew, then hung up. "Okay, that's done. Do they still serve food at this restaurant?"

They ordered and had a second drink while they waited.

"My problem isn't solved," Stone said. "I've got a dinner date with Hilda tomorrow night."

"And you're worried about being the main course?"

"Let's just say that I don't want to be alone with her, and that is what she has in mind."

"Because you'll be found in the Hudson the following morning?" He tapped the signet ring on Stone's little finger. "At least we'll be able to identify you. No gators in the Hudson, last time I checked."

"You're a barrel of laughs," Stone said glumly.

"Your body could be found in a barrel," Dino said. "We get a lot of that."

Dinner came, and Dino ate voraciously, while Stone picked at his food.

"You're not gonna let all this affect your appetite, are you?" Dino asked.

"What appetite?"

"I think I've got a solution to your problem," Dino said.

"What's that?"

"Break your dinner date."

"You think? No kidding?"

"Just become unavailable to her."

"She's pretty persistent," Stone said. "I mean, I became unavailable to her when we flew to England."

"And now she's baaaack!" Dino said.

"What I need is a more permanent solution."

"You already tried that," Dino pointed out.

"Not that permanent; just kind of, for a few weeks or months."

"Do you think her heart will grow less fond of you during that time? Just call her and kiss her off."

"I don't have much experience doing that to women."

"You want me to suggest some language?" Dino asked.

"Spare me that."

Dino looked toward the door. "How do you feel about coincidence?" he asked.

"What?"

"I remember you said something once about,

'If you line up enough coincidences, the result is fate.'"

"I could have said that. It's true, sort of."

"Well, check out the couple being seated across the room, there."

Stone followed Dino's nod to the couple. One of them was Sal Trafficante; the other was Hilda Ross.

"Oh, shit," Stone said.

"That's what I was gonna say," Dino said.

52

The following morning, Stone went to his desk and buzzed Joan.

"Yes, sir?"

"Did you replenish our funds yet?"

"I'm going to the bank this morning."

"All right, in addition to what you were going to get, I'd like two bundles of cash: fifty thousand dollars each."

"Another hundred G's?"

"That's right."

"As you wish." She hung up.

An hour later, Joan returned from the bank and walked into Stone's office. "Where would you like these?" she asked.

"Please gift-wrap one bundle, and shape it like a book," Stone said, "then wrap the other bundle in brown paper the same way and put it in the trunk of the Bentley."

"Okeydokey," she replied, taking the money back to her desk.

Stone's cell rang. "Yes?"

"It's Hilda. I've been rethinking tonight."

"Oh?"

"Yeah. We both know what we want to do to each other, right?"

"You betcha."

"Well, come up to my suite"—she gave him the number—"and we'll rip each other's clothes off and do it right away. Then we can order dinner from room service and start all over again."

"That's a very attractive idea," Stone said. She couldn't murder him in a Carlyle suite and hope to get away with it: too many people around, and body disposal would be particularly difficult. "See you at seven."

They both hung up.

Joan came back with the beautifully gift-wrapped cash. "Looks very fetching, doesn't it?"

"Very much indeed," Stone said.

She held up the brown paper–wrapped package. "And this goes in the trunk?"

"Yes, please."

"Where in the trunk would you like it?"

"Right in the middle, where you couldn't miss it if you opened the trunk."

"Gotcha." She headed off to the garage with the brown bundle.

That night at seven, Stone got out of the Bentley at the Seventy-Sixth Street entrance to the Carlyle, carrying the gift-wrapped package, went up to Hilda's suite, and rang the bell. A moment later, she cracked the door with the chain still on and had a look at him. "You must be the guy," she said.

"I'm the guy."

She closed the door, unhooked the chain, opened it again, then let him in. She was fetchingly dressed, Stone thought, in a silk dressing gown, open at the front from neck to the Mound of Venus. He liked it.

She came close and gave him a soft, wet kiss. "What's in the package?" she asked "A gift for me?"

"Yes," Stone said, "but you'll have to earn it."

"Well," she said, "let's get started on that." She peeled the clothes off of him and draped them neatly over a chair, then picked up the package with one hand, then took hold of Stone's member with the other, and led him into the bedroom, where the bed was already turned down. She set the package on a side table, then dragged Stone onto the bed with her.

For a half hour or so they did everything they

could think of to each other, then they lay, temporarily exhausted, on the bed.

"What would you like for dinner?" Hilda asked.

"A prime New York strip steak, medium, baked potato with a lot of stuff on it, and I'll split a Caesar salad with you."

Hilda picked up the phone and ordered for the two of them. "Wine?" she asked.

"A bottle of Opus One cabernet."

She ordered that. "Dessert?"

"Dessert is you."

She hung up and came back to him. "Now can I open my gift?"

"You haven't earned it, yet," Stone said.

"I thought I earned it pretty well."

"There something you and I have to agree to before you can open it."

"I'm sure I won't have any trouble doing that. What is your pleasure?"

"We have to agree to stop trying to kill each other."

She was silent for half a minute. "Is that what we've been trying to do?"

"You're doing whatever Sal wants you to do, and I sent Cara."

"Why did you send Cara?"

"Because I knew you were going to try to kill me. If we can't agree on this, then I'll get dressed, and you can eat my steak, and we'll go on with what we've been doing. Eventually, one of us will get lucky. It might even be you."

Hilda blinked her long eyelashes. "All right, I'll agree. I won't try to kill you anymore."

"And I agree not to try to kill you."

"I'm glad we got that out of the way," she said. "I feel better. Now, may I open my gift, please?"

"It's not a gift. It's a partial payment for services to be rendered."

"You want to hire me?"

"I do."

"For what purpose?"

"I want you to kill Sal Trafficante."

She looked at him closely. "You're not kidding, are you?"

"I kid you not."

"But you just asked me not to kill anymore."

"Not to kill me. I didn't mention Sal."

"Why Sal?"

"Because he wants to kill me, preferably using your skills, and eventually, he will get lucky. All I've accomplished so far is to disarm him of one weapon: you. He has other weapons at his disposal."

"That, he does."

"But I have a weapon he doesn't know about."

"What is that?"

"Your hatred of him."

She laughed. "You're right, he doesn't know about that."

"Now you can open your package," Stone said. "If you're agreeable to my terms."

"I'll tell you after I see what's inside."

"Fair enough." He tossed her the package.

She sat up, reached for the package, and ripped away the ribbon and paper. "Oh, what good taste you have!"

"It's for the girl who has everything."

"How much is here?"

"Fifty thousand dollars."

"And when Sal is dead?"

"You get another fifty thousand dollars—immediately, no waiting."

"How'm I supposed to kill him?"

"Any method you like; you get to choose."

"For a hundred grand?"

"I hear that's higher than the going rate."

"When am I supposed to do it?"

"Tomorrow evening is convenient."

"'Convenient'? Do you want to watch?"

"No, thanks. You can photograph the body with your iPhone for verification."

"Where's the other half of the hundred grand?"

"It will be readily available in a convenient place. I'll give you directions as soon as you've verified his demise. You'll have the money five minutes later."

"What makes you think I'll do this?"

Stone shrugged. "Hatred is a good motive. So is greed. Also, I think you would enjoy doing it."

"You don't care how I do it?"

"I don't want you to get caught, so be careful. But if you want to tie him up and torture him first, that's okay with me. Oh, it would be nice if you could say to him, while he can still understand, that I ordered his death and hired you."

"What happens if I don't take the job?"

"Then you don't get the hundred grand."

"Not even the first half?"

"This is a business transaction, not your birthday."

"You are a cold, heartless bastard," she said.

"Do you care? I think you'd like to have Sal off your back as much as I."

The doorbell rang, and she grabbed her robe. "Don't get dressed," she said. "I'm not through with you, yet."

"I'm counting on that," Stone said.

She went into the living room, closing the door behind her. When she returned she beckoned him into the living room. The table was set before the windows, looking south, at the carpet of lights that was Manhattan.

"Sit," she said, holding a chair for him.

He sat. "One thing," he said.

"What's that?"

"When you blow out the candles, be careful. Hot wax on naked flesh is painful."

53

Hilda put down her fork. "All right, I'll kill Sal tomorrow night. We already have a date."

"Where are you going for dinner?"

"His place."

"How convenient. Will there be anyone else present at his residence?"

"No. Sal's idea of a good dinner before sex is a pizza from Domino's—the Extravaganza, hold the green peppers."

"An Italian who doesn't like green peppers?"

"He's allergic."

"Allergic enough to kill him?"

"If I could trick him into eating them."

"I think you'd better have a plan B," Stone said.

"I can tuck a straight razor into my garter belt."

"I've never seen you wear a garter belt."

"Sal likes them."

"So do I. I never knew Sal and I had anything in common, except you."

"The nice thing about the straight razor is that it's fast, nearly painless, and the amount of blood rushing out paralyzes the victim with fear."

"Suppose his anger overcomes his fear for a few seconds. How will you handle that?"

"He will weaken almost instantly. I'll be stronger than he. That's how it went with Cara, except I used an ice pick through the back and into the heart."

Stone must have exhibited a moment of revulsion, because she said, "In your shower. All the blood was washed away."

"Excuse me a moment," Stone said. "I have to use your powder room." She pointed, and he found it just in time to vomit neatly into the toilet. So much for the prime beef. He splashed cold water on his face, then slapped himself hard a couple of times, to be sure his face was not drained of color. He returned to the table, looking at his watch. "I have to go," he said.

"Why?"

"To begin to establish my alibi. I was never here, for a start."

"The elevator man will have seen you."

"I took the elevator to two floors below, then walked up. I'll walk down two floors, then ring for the elevator."

"I approve."

Stone got dressed. "It's been fun," he said.

"Sal will be dead by nine o'clock tomorrow evening," Hilda said. "What do I do when I'm done?"

"Send me an e-mail with half a dozen pictures of the body, then erase it from your phone. I'll text you instructions for collecting the cash. My car will appear nearby. Rap twice on the trunk lid, and my driver will open it. The package will be in plain view. Don't concern yourself with him as a witness. The car is armored, as is the glass pane between the front and rear seats, and my driver was the Royal Marines pistol champion, three years running. Once you close the trunk lid, he'll be gone, and you'll be rich—including Cara's 25K. By the way, she made the front page of the **Miami Herald**."

He kissed her softly and left, walking down two flights and ringing for the elevator there.

Fred was waiting with the car. "P. J. Clarke's," Stone said to him.

"Are we on for tomorrow evening?" Fred asked.

"Yes. It will be exactly as we discussed."

Stone got out at Clarke's and found Dino on his second drink.

"Let's go straight in," Stone said. "I'm starved."

"Didn't she give you dinner?" Dino asked.

"In a manner of speaking," Stone replied. "I rejected it."

They ordered.

"How is it going to go?" Dino asked.

"Don't ask me questions you don't want the answer to."

"Don't start with that again. I need to know."

"Why?"

"To cover your ass, if it goes wrong."

"I think it will go as it should."

"Suppose she misses?"

"She's going to use a straight razor."

"Do I need to know where?"

"The medical examiner will explain it to you, in due course," Stone said.

"I have to wait for his report?"

"No, he can tell you on the phone."

"When is this taking place?"

"Before nine o'clock tomorrow evening," Stone said.

"Where?"

"At Trafficante's home. I don't know where that is, and it's just as well you don't, either."

"Is she going to call it in?"

"I doubt it. Would you, given the circumstances?"

"No, I'd get the hell out of there."

"I expect she will, too."

54

Stone was halfway through his morning, when Joan buzzed. "Jack Coulter is here. Once again, he doesn't have an appointment."

"Send him in."

Jack entered and sat down.

"Coffee?" Joan asked.

"Thank you, yes," Jack said.

"I'll pass," Stone replied. "It keeps me awake in the afternoons."

Joan brought a little tray with everything Jack needed.

"I've had an idea," Jack said, when she had gone.

"Tell me."

"I think we should do away with Sal Trafficante, and we should hire Mickey O'Brien to take care of it."

Stone smiled. "What is it they say? Great minds think alike?"

"They do."

"But why Mickey O'Brien?"

"He's skilled at these things, and he always needs the money."

"I thought he had come over all rich, courtesy of his mother."

"He's a degenerate gambler. I'll bet he's already blown it all on a sure thing."

"I don't want to employ Mickey O'Brien, for two reasons: first, I don't trust him. He'd love to have something on me, and I'm not going to give it to him."

"A perfectly good reason. What's your second?"

"I've already made the arrangements."

"Where?"

"At Sal's home. I don't know where it is. I'm leaving that to the contractor."

Jack wrote something on a pad and gave it to Stone. "Here's his address. Memorize it, then shred and burn it."

Stone memorized it, then fed it into the shredder under his desk.

"Who's the contractor?"

"Hilda Ross."

Jack looked surprised "And you trust **her**? Hilda killed Cara, and she knows you sent Cara."

"We've gotten past that," Stone said.

"How does somebody get 'past that'?"

"Greed, for one thing. I'm paying her a hundred thousand, and I've already given her the first fifty. Greed is her motive. That, and her deep hatred for Sal."

"What makes you think she hasn't been hired by Sal to kill you?" Jack asked.

"It would not shock me to hear that Sal had done that, nor that Hilda had taken the contract. She likes money, and she wouldn't mind taking it from both ends of the deal."

"How did you come to this arrangement with Hilda?"

"I saw her last night, in circumstances where it would have been unwise to kill me, and I gave her the first fifty thousand. Then I got the hell out of there, before she could change her mind. I was also repulsed when she told me how she killed Cara."

"Do I want to know?"

"Not unless you want to get sick, but maybe you have a stronger stomach than I."

Jack held up a hand. "No, please. I was fond of the girl."

"That's what I thought."

"So, how is Hilda going to pull this off?"

"She already has a dinner date with him tonight at his place, where he likes to order in pizza from Domino's. I'll leave the rest to her. Oh, she did mention that she'd use a straight razor."

"Then she'd better do it in the bathtub, or she'll have a very messy crime scene on her hands."

"She has some history of working in a bathroom."

Jack threw up both hands this time. "No, don't tell me. I'll never be able to take a bath again."

Stone remembered that he himself had been reluctant to take a shower that morning, but he had handled it.

"How are you going to verify that Sal is dead?"

"She's going to e-mail me photographs."

"I thought you had a weak stomach."

"Strong enough for that," Stone said. "Do you want to see them?"

"It's not my contract, so no. You should erase them immediately, anyway, and restart your phone."

"I'll do that."

"I'll be relieved if this works out," Jack said. "Then I can go back to being a solid citizen."

"More than that, Jack. You're a class act."

"Thank you for that assessment," Jack said, rising, "and for the coffee, too."

"You're very welcome for both," Stone said, shaking his hand.

"Let me know how it goes," Jack said, as he left.

"I will."

55

Stone sat Fred Flicker down and talked to him. "Here's what we need to do," he said.

Fred leaned forward attentively.

"Here's the address where the events of this evening are centered. You don't go inside, but I'd like you to park the car within sight of it, if that is possible. Dinner will be delivered to the house from a Domino's Pizza, presumably from the one closest to the house. That will indicate that the game is afoot. It would be a good time for you to maneuver closer to the house, then call me and give me the exact address where you are parked."

"Right."

"When I get the call, I'll give a woman the address. She will leave the house, find the car, and rap twice on the trunk lid. When that happens, press the button to open it, and she will take a package from the trunk, which is already there.

Then she'll close the lid and walk away. After that you will come home and park in the garage. Got it?"

Fred repeated the sequence of the events. "Got it."

"You should be on site no later than about seven o'clock."

"Plenty of time," Fred said, consulting his watch.

"Off with you, then," Stone said. "Don't ever get out of the car. Take a bottle to pee in, if necessary."

"I understand, sir." Fred let himself out of the office.

Stone met Dino at seven at the Polo Bar, Ralph Lauren's restaurant, on East Fifty-Fifth Street, and they had their first drink at the bar.

"A special occasion?" Dino asked, looking around. It was the first time they had been there together.

"Sort of," Stone said.

"This is an alibi, isn't it?"

"Why do you say that?" Stone asked.

"Because you look like a guy who needs an alibi."

"Stop being so goddamned prescient," Stone said. "I'm where I am, that's all, and in the company of the police commissioner of the City of New York." He looked at his watch. "And it's seven-forty PM."

"Your alibi is established," Dino said. "As long as you don't leave too early."

Ten minutes later, they were shown to their table. Stone had requested one in the bar, so they could better see and be seen. A few minutes later, the mayor came into the restaurant with his wife and another couple. He stopped by their table and spoke to Stone and Dino.

"Dino," he said, "if you can afford to dine here, you're under arrest," said the mayor, a former police commissioner himself.

"He's paying," Dino replied, jerking a thumb toward Stone.

The mayor continued to his own table. "Your alibi is cemented in place," Dino said.

"If I should need one," Stone replied.

At a little past eight o'clock, Stone's iPhone vibrated, and he checked his messages. From Fred: **Domino's arrived and departed.**

Stone deleted the text, then made sure it wasn't in his trash file.

"Everything on schedule?" Dino asked.

"I've no idea what you're talking about," Stone replied.

* * *

Finally, it was ten o'clock, and they were finishing dessert. Stone checked his watch again. His phone vibrated.

Nothing, Fred said.

Are you on site?

Fred gave him the address.

Stone deleted the messages and hung up.

"Everything is not on schedule," Dino said. "What time was it supposed to happen?"

"By nine o'clock," Stone said. "If, indeed, anything was supposed to happen."

Dino put down his spoon and finished his coffee. "Something went wrong," he said. "Let's get out of here."

They went outside and got into Dino's big SUV, where he put up the glass partition separating them from the driver's ears.

"You want to tell me what's not happening?" Dino asked.

"See if anything has been called in from around Tompkins Square Park," Stone said.

Dino called a number and spoke a few words. "And tell them not to touch anything until I get there." He hung up. "Now you're the one who's prescient," he said. He rolled down the partition and gave his driver the address.

Stone texted Fred. **Abort. Go home.**

* * *

They rolled up to Tompkins Square. They had been preceded by two patrol cars, an ambulance, and the medical examiner's wagon.

Dino led the way into the building through the front door, where a patrolman was on guard. There was a Domino's box on the living room coffee table, with a couple of slices left untouched.

"In there," a Detective said to Dino, pointing toward a bedroom.

Dino led the way through the bedroom and into a roomy bathroom that featured a large claw-foot tub that appeared to be filled with blood. They stepped up to the edge and looked down. "That's Sal Trafficante," Stone said quietly to Dino. He knew the woman was Hilda Ross, but he didn't want to be heard saying so.

Sal lay on his back, a cut across his jugular vein just visible. The woman, who was draped over the tub, facedown in the red water, had an ice pick buried in her back, up to the hilt.

"Do you recognize the woman?" Dino asked.

"Nope."

Dino turned to the ME. "Can we see her face without disturbing your scene?"

The ME stepped over, took the body by the hair, and pulled her head up just far enough to reveal her face.

"Know her?" Dino asked Stone.

"Nope."

"Thank you, gentlemen," Dino said. "Continue as you were." He led the way out of the bathroom and the house. When they were about to get into the car, he said, "It was Hilda, right?"

"Maybe," Stone said. "I can't be sure."

Dino snorted and got into the car. "Let's go," he said. "To Barrington's house."

"Not yet," Stone said. "Let's go to the Carlyle."

"To the Carlyle Hotel," Dino said to the driver, then turned toward Stone. "What the fuck for?"

"Burglary," Stone said.

56

Dino's driver parked near the Carlyle's Seventy-Sixth Street entrance. Stone led the way inside, to an elevator without an operator. He took a plastic card from his jacket pocket, inserted it into a slot, then tapped in the number of the floor, two below their destination. Once there, they walked up two flights of stairs, and Stone used the card to let them into Hilda's suite.

"Where'd you get the key card?" Dino asked.

"I stole it when I was here last night." He led the way into the bedroom and opened a closet door, revealing a safe on an upper shelf.

"Hey, wait a minute," Dino said. "Do you know how hard it is to get into a hotel safe without the code? You gotta get a guy up here with a drill, and they end up having to replace the door. We don't need the attention."

Stone reached up, tapped in a code, and the safe opened.

"How'd you do that?" Dino asked.

"I watched her open it last night." He opened the door wide, and it was filled with stacks of bank notes. He found a briefcase, put it on the bed, opened it, and examined the contents. "Nothing of any consequence," he said, emptying the case into a bedside trash basket, then he began removing stacks from the safe and packing them into the briefcase. "Just big enough," he said, closing the case and snapping it shut.

"How much is in there?" Dino asked.

"Seventy-five thousand, give or take."

"Why do you want it?"

"It's mine. And my fingerprints and Joan's are all over it."

They were both frozen in their tracks when a deep voice behind them said, "What the hell are you doing?"

They turned to find a large man standing in the doorway, lit from behind by the living room lights.

Stone let out his breath. "I'm stealing back my money, Jack," he said. "Now what the hell are you doing here?"

"I wanted to go through the place and be sure there's nothing here to incriminate you."

"Trust me, there isn't."

"I know what's happened," Jack said.

"Okay," Dino said. "What's happened, and how do you know about it?"

"Sal and Hilda are both dead, each by the other's hand, it seems."

"Keep going," Dino said.

"Very unusual for two people to off each other simultaneously, but that's what appears to have happened."

"I'll let you know the official position on that after I've heard from the ME," Dino said.

"I'd appreciate that. I'm curious to know."

"How did you get in here?" Stone asked.

"Ancient burglary skills. Thank you for getting the safe open. I don't have that skill, and I was about to call a safecracker."

"Don't mention it," Stone said. "And I mean that. Not to anybody."

"Don't worry."

"Did you find anything incriminating here?" Stone asked.

"No, but I'd wipe the doorknob on your way out."

"Are you staying, Jack?"

"Just for a short time. I'll wipe down any prints I see that are larger than a woman's."

Stone took out his pocket square and wiped down the safe. "Save you the trouble," he said.

"Ready, Dino?"

"There's nothing for me here."

"Then let's go." They left, and Stone wiped

down the doorknob. They walked down two flights, then took the elevator to the lobby and walked back to Dino's cruiser.

"Barrington's house," Dino said to his driver, then rolled up the partition between them. Shortly, they pulled up in front of Stone's house.

"How about a nightcap?" Stone said.

"You talked me into it," Dino replied.

They went into Stone's study, where Stone set the briefcase on the coffee table and then poured them both a cognac.

As they sat down, Fred rapped on the doorjamb. "Excuse me, sir."

"Come in, Fred."

"May I speak to you alone, sir?"

"It's okay. The commissioner is bought and paid for."

"I just wanted to tell you what happened."

"All right."

"I was parked half a block away, and at about eight-fifteen, a Domino's delivery vehicle pulled up, and the driver got out and rang the bell. A man came to the door and the pizza and some money changed hands, then the driver left."

"And then?"

"Nothing. That was it."

"Hear anything?"

"No, sir. Sitting in the Bentley with the motor running, it was pretty quiet."

"Right. That will be all, Fred. Good night."

"Good night, sir," Fred replied, then disappeared.

When he had gone, Dino said. "It's an expensive briefcase. What are you going to do with it?"

"Yes, it's from Hermès, handmade, probably cost eight or ten thousand dollars."

"It would attract too much attention, if you tossed it into a dumpster."

"Good point. Do you want it?"

"I'd like Viv to think that I spent that much money on a birthday gift for her. It's next week."

Stone opened the briefcase, stacked the money inside his concealed safe, then handed the briefcase to Dino. "There you go. Wish her a happy birthday from me."

"Not from you, from me," Dino said, examining the case closely. "Not a mark on it."

"I'd wipe it down with a little saddle soap, inside and out. Can you steal an Hermès box from somewhere?"

"I was counting on you for that."

"I'll have Joan look around. She saves things like that."

"Good idea."

"Anyway, now your lips are sealed."

"What do you mean by that?"

"Now, you're officially an accomplice."

"To what?"

"To anything I might be charged with," Stone said.

57

The following morning Stone felt like running. Normally, he worked out in his home gym, but it was a beautiful day, and Bob could use the workout, too. Besides, for the first time in a while, nobody was trying to kill him. He had tried to interest Bob in the treadmill, but the two had not become friends.

He dressed in his running garb, and put on a belt holding a pouch, into which he put a face-cloth, his phone, some cash, and a small wallet with his driver's license and credit cards, then he clipped Bob's expandable leash to his collar, and they left the house. He went unarmed for the first time in many days.

Stone's gait and Bob's meshed easily, and they both ran at a good lope. They headed uptown and entered Central Park, where Stone took a breather on a park bench, and Bob lay down beside him, panting.

Stone's cell phone rang: **Caller Unknown**. "Hello?"

"Stay where you are," Jack said. "I'm going to come and sit beside you, but don't acknowledge my presence." He hung up before Stone could reply.

Five minutes later, someone sat down at the other end of Stone's park bench and opened a **New York Times**. "Good morning," Jack said.

"Right," Stone said, looking the other way.

"I've some things to tell you," Jack said, "and it's going to take a few minutes. When I'm done, resume your run, and I'll keep reading my paper until you're out of sight."

"How did you know I'd be here?" Stone asked. "I mean, half an hour ago, **I** didn't know."

"I was sitting on my terrace, as I often do, checking out the people in the park with my binoculars, when you ran into my field of vision and sat down. Now, are you ready to listen?"

"Yes," Stone wiped his face and neck with a facecloth from his bag.

"I cleaned up more than the Carlyle suite last night," he said. "I cleaned up Sal Trafficante's house, too, to the extent that it needed cleaning up. Or rather, I had it cleaned, by somebody whose knowledge of police procedure exceeds mine. I'm speaking of Michael O'Brien, who, as I expected, had found the perfect horse and bet big on it. I offered him fifty thousand dollars to kill Sal and Hilda. I took the money to his house and showed it to him, then sent him to Sal's place, which is right around the corner from Michael's. This was about nine-thirty. He called me and told me they were already dead. I told him I'd still give him the money. He said he'd make the crime scene cop-proof, then he returned to his own house, where I had done some things in his absence."

"What sort of things?"

"Mainly, the note."

"Note?"

"Michael had a small, electric typewriter on his desk. I fed in a sheet of his stationery, then typed a note which said, more or less, 'I did both Sal Trafficante and Hilda Ross, because I was afraid of them both. I owed a bookie that belonged to Sal, and I thought he would hire Hilda to kill me. I arranged the crime scene, especially the bodies, then I got out and came home. I had expected to find money in Sal's house, but I didn't, so I came home empty-handed. I'm broke, now, and my mother will disinherit me as soon as she finds out, so I'm doing this for her, so she won't have to have the pain of dealing with me anymore.'

"When Mickey came home I was ready for him. I had long latex gloves on and a bib around my neck, and a plastic face shield on. I pointed a gun at him, sat him down at his desk, took his own weapon from his shoulder holster and, without another word, shot him in the right side of his forehead. His fingerprints were already on the weapon, so I dropped it beside him, stuffed my protective gear into a shopping bag, took my briefcase containing his money and left, disposing of the various pieces of my gear along the route uptown. Questions?"

"Jesus, Jack, why did you do it?"

"Because Mickey O'Brien was still a threat to me. And what's more, I believe Sal hired him, not Hilda, to kill you. Now you and I both are clear of everybody who could have hurt us. I couldn't tell you this last night, because Dino was there. Any other questions?"

"No."

"Then resume your run, and I'll do the crossword."

Stone got up, and so did Bob. They continued their run.

When he got back to his office, he stopped by Joan's desk.

"Good morning. Nice run?" she asked.

"Perfect," Stone said. "Remember all the cash you got from the bank?"

"Yes. I couldn't forget that much money."

"It's in the safe in my study. Please return it to wherever you keep cash. We'll use it as necessary."

"Is the money anything to do with this?" she asked, handing him a **Daily News** with a photo of Sal Trafficante on the front page.

"Jesus!" Stone said, reading the piece while faking surprise. "No, it's nothing to do with this."

She looked at him askance. "Whatever you say, boss."

58

Jack Coulter continued to work on his **Times** crossword until it was finished, then he got up and walked from his bench out into Grand Army Plaza. As he strolled past the fountain in front of the Plaza Hotel, a car with darkened windows pulled up beside him, and the rear door opened. The driver got out and something hard pressed into Jack's gut, and he was propelled into the car. His upper body was quickly frisked, then the door was closed firmly behind him, and the driver got back into the car. It began to move.

"Good morning, Johnny," the elderly, well-dressed man beside him said.

"Good morning, Don Antonio," he replied. "To what do I owe this, ah, invitation?"

"It is time for us to speak," the Don said, lapsing into his native Sicilian dialect. "Much has happened, much has changed. I know of your part in these changes."

Jack didn't bother asking how he knew. "I see," he said.

"Most of these changes had to be done, in any case, but you were useful in implementing them, particularly the departure of Salvatore."

"I didn't send him the girl," Jack said.

"Please," the Don said, "lying between us is offensive. Let us be frank with each other."

"As you wish, Don Antonio."

"I admire the manner in which you have caused yourself to disappear."

Jack said nothing.

"I might not have known, had it not been for Michael O'Brien, and you, very kindly, arranging for him to disappear into the city morgue."

Jack kept quiet.

"It is time for a new beginning," the Don said. "I am old, and if I am careful and fortunate, I will live, perhaps another two years—or possibly, less, according to the Mayo Clinic, where I have recently undergone a complete evaluation. I could, perhaps, stretch that for another year or two, but it would require major surgery. And the recovery time could be weeks, perhaps even months, and I would be incapacitated for much of that time. I prefer to live out my natural life with my wits about me. I hope you can understand that."

"Of course," Jack replied. "It is what I would wish for myself."

"Because of recent events a vacancy exists in my family which cannot be filled from inside it, because of a lack of suitable talent. I invite you to become a member of my family, and to fill that vacancy, recently occupied by Salvatore."

Jack became hyper alert. If he did not manage the next couple of minutes well, his body might never be found. Certainly, a resting place for it had already been found and awaited him.

He reflected in a space of seconds that this was the man who had kept him in prison long after he could have been paroled, just so that his sister's son could serve his time in safety.

"You honor me, Don Antonio," Jack said finally. "I gratefully accept your invitation."

The Don let out a long breath, as if he had been holding it. He pressed a button, and the partition between the passengers and the driver lowered a few inches. The Don began rattling off directions to the driver. The car slid to a stop, and Jack could see ahead of them. The car was on an empty street on the West Side, a block from the Hudson.

"And after that," the Don said, then continued with his instructions.

Jack crossed his legs and hoisted his left trouser leg. He pulled down his sock, and a .22 semi-automatic pistol fell into his hand. He reached out and shot the driver twice in the head, then he swiveled toward the Don. "I lied," he said. Then he shot the man once in the head, causing him to fall sideways, then fired a second shot.

Jack opened the car door, got out, and walked downhill toward the river, fighting the urge to hurry. There was a car wash to his left, on Twelfth Avenue, and a taxi pulled out of it. Jack flagged him down and got in, noting that there was no chase car behind the Don's vehicle. "Central Park and Fifty-Ninth Street," he said to the driver, then settled back for the ride, his mind racing.

Gradually, he relaxed. There had been no entourage to witness his departure from the park or the Don's car. The Don had been that confident of him.

"Let me out at the Plaza," he said to the driver. When they arrived there, he paid the man, got out of the cab, and walked into the hotel lobby. He spent a couple of minutes window-shopping the little boutiques, then, satisfied that no one was following him, left the hotel in the direction of the fountain, then walked for another half hour before he felt confident that he was still alone. He reduced the small pistol to its parts and threw them into dumpsters along his route, then he took a taxi further downtown.

* * *

Stone was at his desk when Joan buzzed. "Yes?"

"Jack Coulter is here," she said. "He doesn't have an appointment."

Jack entered Stone's office, with Joan and his coffee close behind.

"Good morning, Jack."

"Good morning, Stone."

"What brings you to see me so soon after our earlier encounter?"

"I have news. Its source, let us say, is from my personal grapevine."

"Uh-oh," Stone said. "Now what?"

"When I told you that, with Sal Trafficante dead, you and I had no further worries about assassins, I believed that to be true, at the time, but I had reckoned without Don Antonio Datilla."

Stone slumped.

"We have nothing to fear from the Don. A short time ago, he and his driver were shot dead in his car on the West Side, near the car wash."

Stone's eyes widened. "Who would take on the Don?"

Jack shrugged. "Someone who, with Sal gone, no longer feared him. He was, after all, an old man, not well, and he had no one left he could trust. There was a break in his shield, and someone took advantage of it."

"Any idea who?"

Jack shrugged again. "I have few acquaintances

among his younger associates. No one comes to mind."

Stone looked sharply at Jack. "No one? Truly?"

"Truly," Jack said. He polished off his coffee and stood. "Well, with my news imparted, I will be going."

Stone stood with him and shook his hand. "Where are you off to?"

Jack smiled. "Anywhere I like," he said.

END

January 30, 2021
Key West, Florida

AUTHOR'S NOTE

I am happy to hear from readers, but you should know that if you write to me in care of my publisher, three to six months will pass before I receive your letter, and when it finally arrives it will be one among many, and I will not be able to reply.

However, if you have access to the Internet, you may visit my website at www.stuartwoods.com, where there is a button for sending me e-mail. So far, I have been able to reply to all my e-mail, and I will continue to try to do so.

If you send me an e-mail and do not receive a reply, it is probably because you are among an alarming number of people who have entered their e-mail address incorrectly in their mail software. I have many of my replies returned as undeliverable.

Remember: e-mail, reply; snail mail, no reply.

When you e-mail, please do not send attachments, as I never open these. They can take twenty minutes to download, and they often contain viruses.

Please do not place me on your mailing lists for funny stories, prayers, political causes, charitable fund-raising, petitions, or sentimental claptrap. I get enough of that from people I already know. Generally speaking, when I get e-mail addressed to a large number of people, I immediately delete it without reading it.

Please do not send me your ideas for a book, as I have a policy of writing only what I myself invent. If you send me story ideas, I will immediately delete them without reading them. If you have a good idea for a book, write it yourself, but I will not be able to advise you on how to get it published. Buy a copy of **Writer's Market** at any bookstore; that will tell you how.

Anyone with a request concerning events or appearances may e-mail it to me or send it to: Putnam Publicity Department, Penguin Random House LLC, 1745 Broadway, New York, NY 10019.

Those ambitious folk who wish to buy film, dramatic, or television rights to my books should contact Matthew Snyder, Creative Artists Agency, 2000 Avenue of the Stars, Los Angeles, CA 90067.

Those who wish to make offers for rights of a literary nature should contact Anne Sibbald, Janklow & Nesbit, 285 Madison Avenue, 21st

Floor, New York, NY 10017. (Note: This is not an invitation for you to send her your manuscript or to solicit her to be your agent.)

If you want to know if I will be signing books in your city, please visit my website, www.stuartwoods.com, where the tour schedule will be published a month or so in advance. If you wish me to do a book signing in your locality, ask your favorite bookseller to contact his Penguin representative or the Penguin publicity department with the request.

If you find typographical or editorial errors in my book and feel an irresistible urge to tell someone, please write to Sara Minnich at Penguin's address above. Do not e-mail your discoveries to me, as I will already have learned about them from others.

A list of my published works appears in the front of this book and on my website. All the novels are still in print in paperback and can be found at or ordered from any bookstore. If you wish to obtain hardcover copies of earlier novels or of the two nonfiction books, a good used-book store or one of the online bookstores can help you find them. Otherwise, you will have to go to a great many garage sales.

STUART WOODS is the author of ninety novels. He is a native of Georgia and began his writing career in the advertising industry. **Chiefs**, his debut in 1981, won the Edgar Award. An avid sailor and pilot, Woods lives in Key West, Mount Desert Island, and Washington Depot, Connecticut.

STUARTWOODS.COM
FACEBOOK.COM/
STUARTWOODSAUTHOR

LIKE WHAT YOU'VE READ?

Try these titles by Stuart Woods,
also available in large print:

Double Jeopardy
ISBN 978-0-593-39562-2

Jackpot
ISBN 978-0-593-41416-3

Hush-Hush
ISBN 978-0-593-29544-1

For more information on large print titles, visit
www.penguinrandomhouse.com/large-print-format-books